Katelyn was about to face the truth.

The sounds of voices stopped her. She moved closer to the door and peeked inside, not wishing to interrupt anything. A kerosene lamp cast light over the stalls, which housed several quiet horses. She caught sight of the men apparently in deep conversation.

Suddenly Katelyn felt like an intruder. She twirled around to make her departure. James's words stopped her cold.

"I didn't know love would be this way," he confided to his friend.

"That's the way of love, young fella," answered John, sorting through a pile of horseshoes.

"Was it this miserable for you the first time you fell in love?"

"Ah," said John, squaring his shoulders at James. "Was both miserable and confusin'. Weren't prepared any better'n you. The woman filled my head day and night. Found it hard to work, to eat, to sleep."

"Yeah, that's the feeling," James agreed, holding his hand above the heat rising from the top of the lantern.

"Who's got yer heart, fella? If ya don't mind my askin'."

Katelyn felt her own heart race inside her chest. This was the moment of truth, when she would discover whom James loved.

KELLY R. STEVENS is a multipublished, award-winning author of historical and contemporary novels. She spent a portion of her writing career as a journalist and is president of Creative Artisan's Network.

HEARTSONG PRESENTS

Books by Kelly R. Stevens
HP106—Ragdoll

Song
of the Cimarron

Kelly R. Stevens

Heartsong Presents

To Kelleen Patricia, my daughter.
You are a true warrior and an inspiration to my life daily.

Thanks for your help and support during the writing of this
book: Carol David, Grant Johnson, Kelleen Patricia,
and Doris and Virgil Varner.

A note from the author:
*I love to hear from my readers! You may correspond with me
by writing:*

**Kelly R. Stevens
Author Relations
PO Box 719
Uhrichsville, OH 44683**

ISBN 1-57748-479-7

SONG OF THE CIMARRON

Cover illustration by Lauraine Bush.

PRINTED IN THE U.S.A.

one

April 1874

Katelyn wiped her brow with the back of one hand and glanced over at the setting sun, a fiery orb dropping behind the Texas prairie. A cool spring breeze skirted the sweat along her forehead and neck, providing much needed relief. The notes to "Home Sweet Home," her father's favorite song, rose and fell within her throat like a grief-stricken melody. The breeze carried the beautiful words far away, where nobody could hear them.

Completing the final verse to the song, she then recited the Twenty-third Psalm, "Yea though I walk through the valley of the shadow of death. . ." Katelyn carried on methodically, reciting the words just as she remembered them from past services for deceased relatives.

This was too much pain for her young mind to absorb. Another tear coursed down her dirty cheek. She thought she was spent of tears, having cried so much over the last few weeks. *God help me!* Katelyn wanted to scream. *I'm alone. I don't know what to do!*

She rested her gaze on the two crudely made crosses posted into the ground at the head of each grave. A younger brother and now her father had both succumbed to the dreaded smallpox.

Coyotes yelped in the distance, as though in mourning. Katelyn realized they were closer than usual. She needed to pile rocks on the graves soon. But she was so tired, exhausted from hours upon hours of caring for her loved ones at their sickbeds, then having to bury them when they died. After shoveling the last bit of dirt over her father's resting place, she turned and plodded wearily back to the soddie.

When she entered the dark, musty dwelling, she heard her mother moaning. Both Katelyn's mother, Abigail, and Carolyn, her baby sister, had come down with the inflamed red splotches all over their bodies. Resembling boils, several of the sores had popped. A foul-smelling pus oozed from them. High fevers caused delirium.

Katelyn shivered and moved to add more buffalo chips to the fireplace. That accomplished, she stepped to where her mother and tiny sister lay together on the bed her parents had shared before the nightmare began.

"What am I going to do, Lord?" she whispered into the air as she studied their writhing bodies. A lump formed in her throat and a heaviness she couldn't explain threatened to weigh her down.

I am with you, a voice seemed to say.

Katelyn felt too numb to draw peace from it. "Where?" she screamed. "Where are You?"

Gathering a small dose of composure, she filled the ladle from the water bucket and sat next to her mother and Carolyn on the feather ticking.

"Katelyn Patricia," her mother groaned as Katelyn lifted the fevered head with one hand while trickling water into the woman's mouth with the other. Most of the fluid found its way down her chin and onto the flimsy pale blue flannel nightgown that did little to keep her warm.

"I'm here, Mother. Right here."

Abigail opened her eyes to reveal glassy green irises, eyes that peered but didn't see. "Where's Jacob?" she asked, her voice tremulous. "Supper's on. Call the others." With that, she fell back into a disease-ridden slumber.

Katelyn stroked her mother's long, wavy, chestnut hair, her bottom lip quivering. It was she, Katelyn, who resembled her mother. Little Carolyn, or Carrie as she was affectionately called, took more after their father's side of the family.

This pleased Katelyn because her mother was an extremely

gifted woman, known as the healer. She was well respected in their community and beyond. Katelyn thought looking like her mother might create similarities in other ways, ways she could accept.

At nineteen, Katelyn had blossomed into womanhood. To her dismay, she still didn't know her purpose for being. She believed she was the only person alive who hadn't yet discovered her God-given talent.

All her friends seemed to know what they wanted in life. Her lack of direction made Katelyn edgy. If only she had something on which to focus her energies. Feelings of inadequacy surfaced time and again.

She remembered the talk her mother initiated nearly a month ago.

They sat at the pine table made from split logs fastened together with pegs. Everybody else had gone to bed. Her mother had peered at Katelyn over the light of a lard oil lamp. Katelyn felt her chest constrict; her heart beat rapidly. *Am I in trouble?*

"Daughter," her mother had said. "It's time we talk."

"About what, Mama? Have I done something wrong?"

"No, no, no, sweetheart." Abigail cleared her throat, as if what she had to say might be difficult.

She smiled, and Katelyn felt her mother's green eyes warming and calming her like an early summer day.

"You are a woman now," Abigail continued. "And a gifted woman at that."

The heat of confusion rushed into Katelyn's cheeks, flushing them red. "Th–thank you."

"Do you understand your gift?" Abigail asked. "Are you ready to accept it?"

Accept what?

Abigail pressed on, her voice low. "People need what the Lord has given you to offer." She hesitated. "It's the same gift He chose to bestow on me."

Katelyn knew this to be true but fought against the idea.

Although the town of Cimarron had a doctor, Katelyn's mother was called on regularly to assist in medical situations. She knew nearly every herb indigenous to the region, their names and purposes. When trading season came each year, Abigail stayed busy gathering herbs and discovering new medicinal properties in their uses. She shared them with various Indian tribes that migrated west during the season, and they in turn gave her new herbs and remedies unknown to the area.

Unfortunately, the Red River Wars under the command of General Philip H. Sheridan had put a halt to trading. Wars with the Indians blazed a vile path through the Texas Panhandle. The army planned to subdue the Indians once and for all. This would allow settlers to stake claim to land and live in peace.

Regardless of difficult circumstances, Katelyn knew her mother had found her place in the world. And Katelyn knew that she, too, had a knack for medicine. She'd watched her mother and learned much from her. It seemed this was a gift passed down to the women on her mother's side of the family. Katelyn's grandmother was a healer who learned the practice from an Apache woman who had married a distant uncle of French heritage.

Katelyn had overheard relatives and friends conversing with her mother, saying things like, "That girl of yours is just like you when it comes to medicine" or "I hope Katelyn soon realizes her ability with plants and doctoring folks."

Katelyn ignored these comments. She wanted her own gift, something uniquely hers. And that's what she told her mother when her mother had encouraged her to accept the ability she had for healing.

Abigail's voice softened with understanding. "I know you think this gift belongs solely to me. That's not true. Your gift, though like mine in many ways, will develop its own qualities. No two people are alike, nor are any two gifts."

Katelyn hadn't thought of it that way before. Still, she wondered what a town would do with a doctor and two healers.

Maybe she could move away and practice in another town, a community that needed her.

No, she reasoned, *I love Cimarron. It's all I know. I can't leave my family, friends, all the comforts I've grown used to.*

Her voice trembled when she spoke. "Mama, I just don't understand some things. I've seen girls, rich girls, and all they ever need in life is money. They're happy. They're also beautiful. They find husbands and have families easily. I have to work for my place, my dreams. They don't. It doesn't seem fair."

"What is to be gained by looking beautiful?" her mother replied. "Fleshly beauty is a gift, I believe, but it's not eternal. What's genuinely important must come from inside. That's what will endure through time. You must not worry yourself so over appearances."

She paused, as though considering her next words. "I've seen envy in your eyes when you catch sight of some of the women in town. Envy has no place in the heart of a Christian, man or woman. What will those women have to look back on if they rely on beauty alone? Soon that will fade. Then what?"

Katelyn had witnessed the girls at the socials with their fancy flounce dresses, velvet bonnets, and white-gloved hands. They were beautiful, especially Martha Appleburg. Scores of male admirers consistently pressed in on them, vying for attention. It seemed to Katelyn she might go unnoticed indefinitely.

Martha stood out, as far as she was concerned. To Katelyn, Martha epitomized everything a woman should be: beautiful, wealthy, popular. Nor could Katelyn seem to staunch the envy of which her mother spoke. She, herself, was none of those things and could only dream of what such a life must be like.

"True beauty comes from inside," her mother repeated. "Always concentrate on that, what's inside you, Daughter."

"I will try," Katelyn promised, knowing the words made

perfect sense. Applying them was the hard part.

"Then it will last. Outer beauty will someday fade away, but if you work hard on what's inside and follow the Bible's teachings, you will *always* be beautiful."

"Like you, Mama." Reaching across the table, she squeezed her mother's hand. The woman always had a knack for making her feel valuable, special—despite poverty or awkwardness.

Abigail returned the squeeze. "Now, off to bed with you. We've chores to do early in the morning. I've got to help Pa put cheesecloth along the ceiling before the rains come and then I have wash to do."

"I'll help."

"Good girl," Abigail said. "I'm so very proud of you. Now, get along to bed."

Rising, Katelyn stepped to where her mother sat and surrounded her in a gentle hug. "I love you, Mama. Good night."

Suddenly, Katelyn heard a loud wail, ripping her from those warm, peaceful memories. A knot formed in her throat.

Carrie screamed again and clawed at her sores. Their mother seemed to struggle out of her slumber. Briefly she touched her youngest daughter's tear-soaked face.

"Shhh," she said. "Mama's here, baby. Mama's here."

Shivering, Carrie squirmed beneath the quilt and scooted her frail, four-year-old body closer to her mother. She sought the warmth Abigail's body might provide.

Feeling helpless, Katelyn stepped to the window and studied the night through tear-blurred vision. The blackness seemed almost palpable. It frightened her. Only a milky sliver of moon glowed among the throngs of stars flung against the ebony sky like confetti at a carnival.

Her mother and sister hadn't eaten in days. *What can I feed them? Will they even eat?* Maybe some cornmeal mush or some type of pudding. *Yes! Pudding!*

That would mean a trip to the dugout, their crude first

home that had been carved into the prairie hillside. She'd need potatoes. Also eggs from the chicken coop.

Katelyn rubbed her forehead, then dried her eyes and moved to do what she must. Unlatching the front door, she made her exit and trudged nearly twenty yards to the dugout. When she reached the opening, she paused and studied the dwelling. The entire family had lived in its shelter for the better part of two years before the larger sod home was built. Now they used the dugout for storing root crops and vegetables, dried meat, and wild fruit preserves that fed them through the winter months.

The windows had been removed to use in the new soddie, and the openings were boarded up for better insulation. The roof was made of crisscrossed willow and cottonwood poles and topped with a mixture of grass and brush. Katelyn had helped apply the final layer of sod over the grasses and poles. The memory warmed her, bringing thoughts of the time when her family first arrived at this tiny frontier town of Cimarron, forging a new life.

Shaking herself, Katelyn struggled with her thoughts, believing all was lost, all hopes and dreams dying one by one as she buried each family member. Carrie's wails echoed through the night, and Katelyn knew she must hurry. Numbly, she gripped a piece of muslin cloth from a shelf to her right and stumbled to a darkened corner of the room. A barrel half-full with potatoes rested against the earthen wall. Methodically Katelyn grabbed several potatoes and put them on the cloth. She tugged the four corners upward, clenching them in one hand. After a visit to the chicken pen, where she gathered several eggs, she hurried back to the two members of her family she had left.

Carrie screamed in agony, flailing at the saturated sheets and heavy quilt that covered her, searching frantically for comfort. Their mother seemed to have slipped off into another deep slumber where she couldn't even hear her baby's cries.

Knowing she could do little for her sister, Katelyn began preparing food. Having something in her stomach might provide the child some measure of comfort.

After peeling the potatoes, Katelyn quartered them. She dropped the vegetables into the heated water that filled the black iron pot dangling from a pivoting crane over the fire in the hearth. They would need to boil. Katelyn kept heated water at all times, never knowing when she might need it since the sickness set upon her family.

Next, she beat five eggs to a stiff froth. To this she added about a half pound of white sugar, nearly the last of their supply.

As she worked, Katelyn sang. Carrie loved singing. The more Katelyn's voice stretched with familiar melodies, the less the girl cried.

When the potatoes grew soft, Katelyn transferred them from the kettle to a pottery bowl. After mashing them to a very fine consistency, she added the bulk of the eggs and sugar. When this had been mixed well, she retrieved a cast-iron skillet from a shelf in the kitchen lean-to and poured the mixture into it. Removing the huge pot of water from over the fire, she secured the skillet directly over the coals and covered it with a metal lid.

While the pudding baked, Katelyn cracked more eggs into the bowl and separated the yolks. After beating the egg whites to a froth, she added the remainder of the sugar. This would serve as icing to top the potato pudding.

Hopefully, the dish would be tempting enough that her mother and sister might eat. After struggling to spoon-feed the two for nearly an hour, Katelyn relented. She left the food on the pine table for later use. At least she made enough, she reasoned, that it could feed them all for a day or two.

Katelyn struggled to eat, knowing she would need nourishment to make it through the next day. Before she could complete her meal, Carrie wailed again. Stepping to the tiny girl's side, Katelyn bent over her.

"Shh, little one," she soothed while lifting Carrie's sweaty body from the bed. "We have to change your clothes."

"Mama," she cried. "I want my mama."

Katelyn marveled that Carrie was semiconscious, but she wouldn't allow herself to hope for something that might not come to pass. She was almost certain this small child would be next. It was only a matter of time. She could only keep her comfortable until the end came. And her mother. Then what?

She held her sister for nearly an hour until the little one lapsed into another deep sleep. After securing her back on the bed, Katelyn covered her with a dry corner of the damp patchwork quilt. Next she sought dry garments from the Saratoga trunk at the foot of the bed. She found two cotton nightshirts, one for her mother and one for Carrie. Reaching inside the trunk again, she tugged out a pair of homemade slippers, something her mother knitted for Carrie during the winter.

After locating fresh undergarments, Katelyn dropped the creaking lid on the trunk and stepped to her sister's side. When she touched Carrie's arm to remove the damp gown, she drew back instantly, her eyes wide with alarm. Fever! She must bring it down quickly.

Dashing to the kitchen lean-to, she grabbed a jar from one of the cupboards. It held a mixture of turpentine and skunk grease. She massaged the smelly concoction onto Carrie's chest, back, sides—even the soles of her feet. She didn't know why it worked or how, but her mother always used it to fight fevers. Katelyn was glad she'd paid attention, albeit grudgingly, and accepted the knowledge her mother so patiently imparted. She certainly needed that knowledge now.

Carrie struggled to break free as though in severe pain. Katelyn thought the ointment probably burned the boil-like lesions covering her body, but it had to be applied. With the salve glistening on Carrie's tiny body, Katelyn dressed the child in the clean nightshirt and slippers, then wrapped her snugly in a fresh quilt.

Last, she forced water down Carrie's throat, despite the sobbing, then laid her near the hearth where the fire could warm her and ease the shivering. She followed the same procedure with her mother and was pleased the woman didn't fight.

Tasks completed, she stepped to the hearth and lifted her tiny sister from the floor. Katelyn settled into the nearby slat-backed rocker where the tiny fire could cast its warmth over them both. She rocked and sang to Carrie until her voice cracked. The child slept. Between the dying fire and the warmth of Katelyn's body, Carrie soon stopped shaking.

Katelyn grew sleepy, a restless kind of tired. For a time she sat mesmerized by the glowing embers, feeling as though they fought against the cold that would soon overtake them, a coldness she knew firsthand. Her heart was like one of those embers, losing its warmth, its life.

She would never forget this feeling, a feeling death brought with its unyielding sense of loss. She offered a prayer in her desperation.

"Dear Father in heaven, please bring someone to help us. I can't leave my family for one minute. I fear I might lose them if I ventured to get help. In Jesus' name I pray, Amen."

After nearly twenty-four hours with little food and no rest, Katelyn slept. She never felt her eyes close.

two

The inside of the huge barn droned with music and laughter as dancers kept beat to fiddles, harmonicas, and banjos. Others feasted on ham, turkey, beef, pickled oysters, and custard laid out on crudely built tables. Coffee, corn liquor, and fine wine made the rounds in plentiful doses.

James and Martha, breathless, scooted off the dance floor to an unoccupied bale of hay. Tunes to "Little Brown Jug," "Dixie's Land," and "Jeanie with the Light Brown Hair" played in the background.

Martha tapped her chest lightly with slender fingers while heaving for sufficient breath. "Mercy," she finally gasped with a sultry southern accent. "I don't believe I've ever danced as much as I have tonight!" She gazed adoringly at James. "And with such a handsome companion as yourself."

A half-grin played on James's lips. "I'm the fortunate one," he teased, taking all of Martha in with one mild glance. She was a splendid sight in her dark green silk dress, secured at the bodice by large silver buttons and plumped in the rear with a bustle. Lace accents at the neckline and wrists added to the beauty of the latest Paris fashion.

Having been raised and educated back East, James took a fancy to rich society women, finding them amusing. He grew up around them. At age twenty, it was all he knew. To him, they all seemed the same: wealthy and spoiled but *so* much fun.

Before moving to Cimarron, Texas, James's mother and father had run a successful clothing shop in St. Louis, Missouri. The bulk of their business came from wealthy women and their daughters. James got to know many of the daughters quite well.

Then, when James was fourteen, his father decided he

wanted to move west for the adventure. Everybody was doing it. His mother was against the idea, believing she would lose everything: wealth, fame, membership in the women's organizations in which she was heavily invested. It would mean starting completely over. But James's father had had his way. He knew he could never make a fancy clothing shop work on the frontier, but he could use his expertise at managing that business to open a mercantile.

Having sold the clothing store, James's father owed the bank nothing. Their family traveled in style and comfort. James had to admit his mother never seemed to settle down after they arrived, never accepted her new life. But he had.

"It's very considerate of your father and mother to throw this wonderful party for the entire town," James said to Martha, shaking himself from the brief memory. He knew what Martha's response would be before she uttered a word.

"It's not as though they can't afford it. Besides, practically everybody helped with father's barn-raising."

True, James thought, *but who wouldn't have helped support the wealthiest man in Cimarron?* Martha's father, Gabe Appleburg, owned the town's bank and had done well in cattle. He needed a larger barn now that his cattle empire had burgeoned.

It seemed Texans everywhere were getting into livestock and doing quite well with it. Not as well as Gabe Appleburg. Gabe had the funds to finance his side business, while others had only time.

And Gabe was Connor Mercantile's best customer. James and his father needed more customers like the Appleburgs. That's the only way the store thrived. The Appleburgs paid their tabs on time and never needed favors—not that James and his father minded giving favors. Every business thrived on the greenback, though, and theirs was no exception.

"I'm surprised the Fontannas didn't show," Martha said, a pouty smile curving her full lips. "Not one of them! How absolutely rude!" Then under her breath she added, "We'll have to make sure *that* never happens again."

James was constantly amazed at the way Martha's mind worked. Sometimes he was fascinated with her; sometimes dismayed, even bored. His father had asked when he meant to propose like a true gentleman, having courted Martha for eleven months. James had no answer to give. Why? He didn't know.

"Maybe they'll show up late," he suggested.

Laughter rushed out from deep in Martha's throat. "Nobody shows up late for one of *Father's* parties."

"Were they invited?" James tried not to show his agitation. Sometimes this woman could be so self-centered, one thing he *didn't* like about her.

"Everybody was invited, James. You know that." Martha drew in a deep breath. Turning to face James, she smiled beguilingly, her eyes beckoning. She let the breath out with a heated rush when her dance partner apparently failed to notice her intent or pretended not to.

James searched the barn for any sign of the Fontannas. They were good people. He didn't want malicious gossip spread about them if it could be avoided. Martha was good for getting the word around town. She alienated people that way. He couldn't understand that side of her. There were other sides he couldn't appreciate about her either, but, well, she was beautiful. He had a penchant for beautiful women.

Lately, though, one thing continually rubbed his conscience raw. Something was missing in Martha and many other women he had known. He couldn't identify the missing part. Perhaps this was simply part of the makeup of every woman walking the earth. He'd never known different. Yet, he found himself not wanting to believe this to be true.

James had begun to feel a certain discontentment with his life. His father's words floated back to him, as clearly as the music humming in his ears.

"James," he had stated while stocking a shelf with sacks of flour and cans of green corn, "life is not all fun and games. Sometimes—no, mostly—it's hard work. The responsibilities of being a man will soon rest upon your shoulders like a heavy burden."

His father then spoke the words James wasn't prepared to hear. Or was he?

"You'll have to take a wife soon and have younguns to carry on the family name. There's a certain satisfaction that'll come of your labors, and it'll make life seem less of a burden. You'll know peace and joy."

James grew agitated.

"You'll have to lead the family in the ways of the Lord as well. Do all things with Him in your heart, and you can't go wrong."

Then his father had stopped his task and turned around to face James squarely. "It's time you accept your responsibilities and begin acting on them."

A shiver ran up James's spine, and he shoved the memory aside. Of course, he knew his father was right. Ironically that knowledge coincided with his newfound restlessness. He faced Martha.

"I don't see your little sister here," he said.

Tugging at a golden ringlet, Martha smiled, her blue eyes glistening. "Baby sister took ill this morning—bad cold or something." Her smile broadened. "Pity she couldn't make it."

Did he detect mockery in her tone? "I'm sorry to hear that. Has the doctor been to see her yet?"

"Father plans calling on him first thing in the morning. With all the festivities, poor little Maggie will just have to wait."

"I see."

Martha touched him lightly on the shoulder. "Now, James, don't take that the way it sounded." Her lips formed a pout. She touched her nose to his cheek. "You're always taking me wrong." She pulled back. "By the way, where's your father? He was invited, too!"

Worry creased James's forehead. With finger and thumb, he massaged his left temple.

"He came down with something last night," James answered. "Said he wasn't feeling well 'round supper time. Couldn't eat much. Talked about feeling cold, chilled. Thought maybe he was running a low fever."

"Maybe he's got what Maggie has."

Martha seemed to study the people milling around them. James knew she wasn't attentive to his concerns.

Clearing his throat, he said, "I'd best be getting home." Before, he hadn't thought twice about his father not feeling well. Everybody got sick on occasion. Now he was worried. Could one or more of the Fontanna family be down with it, whatever *it* was?

"Oh! Don't go, James! The night's only just begun!" Martha threw him a seductive wink. "I can sneak us some corn liquor, and we could steal off to the loft." She laughed. "Nobody'd be the wiser. It'd be fun. Come on, James!"

James wasn't in any mood for that kind of fun. He'd been raised in a proper Christian home. Much of the teachings had rubbed off on him. Though he couldn't say he was a devout Christian, the words of the Bible lent him a conscience he couldn't deny. He'd rather follow that inner voice that spoke to him at the most inopportune times than deal with the guilt that followed if he didn't heed the warnings. Right now, he had other things to worry about than Martha. If his father wasn't better by morning, he'd have to open the store alone. He'd need rest.

"No, I really need to go," he insisted.

"Well, then go!" Martha pouted childishly.

Irritated, James rose from the hay bale. What exactly did he see in her anyhow? he wondered. She could have any man within a hundred miles if she wanted. Why him? He couldn't remember who pursued whom in the beginning. There was something missing from this relationship, and James knew it had everything to do with why he hadn't proposed marriage.

Bending low, he placed a well-aimed kiss on her pouting

lips, lips that didn't return the gift. "Have a wonderful time, Martha."

"Oh, I will," she answered, raising one glossy eyebrow. "You can bet your last shiner on that!"

Heaving a breath infused with exasperation, James tipped his Stetson at two giggling young ladies walking past, then turned to leave.

Outside, the stars sparkled with brilliance in the black sky. James inhaled the fresh air as he climbed atop his horse, a gelding paint he'd broken only months ago. Clicking his tongue on the roof of his mouth and laying the reins across the horse's neck, he headed home. Within twenty minutes he had reached their barn.

After stabling the horse in its stall, he made his way through the mercantile and into the living quarters, a dark frame dwelling attached to the back of the store. Closing the door behind him, he stopped for a brief second. James couldn't see a thing, but he could hear his father's labored breathing. The fire, started earlier, had completely died out.

Feeling his way, he lit several peg lamps along the walls and located the kerosene lamp on the coffee table closest to the settee in the front room. Once lit, the lamps provided adequate light.

Quietly James made his way to his father's room, the room the older man had, for many years, shared with his mother. James was an only child. The sight caused a painful memory to stir.

He remembered the day he turned fifteen and his mother learned she was pregnant. Although expecting a baby so late in their years was a surprise, his parents were thrilled to have a second child on the way. When the time came to deliver, neither James's mother nor his unborn brother could handle the rigors of labor. She breathed her last breath first. The infant was stillborn minutes later.

The doctor said, "If Emma could have held on fifteen minutes longer, they both would have survived." James nearly choked. She'd been in labor for two hard days. Fifteen more minutes?

Brushing the memory from his mind, he leaned over the four-poster bed and pressed his face close to his father's cheek. The older man's breath was shallow. James touched his forehead with the back of one hand. His father was hot with fever; his skin, dry.

Stepping to the chamber set against the north wall of the room, James gripped the large-mouthed pitcher and poured water into the basin. Next, he retrieved some toweling from the kitchen and returned. He dipped the cloth in the cool water. After ringing out the excess moisture, he hurried to his father's side. Gently, he placed the wet cloth on the sleeping man's forehead. Isaac stirred and moaned incoherently.

"Father," James whispered, his heart beating hard in his chest. "Wake up, Father." *Are you all right?* James wondered. With a fever this high, he'd need fluids. James was ill-prepared to care for a sick person. Others usually took care of that chore.

When Isaac didn't budge, James gripped him by the shoulders with strong hands and shook him. Slowly the man opened his eyes.

"J–James," he mumbled. "Sick, very sick."

"I'm gonna get Doc Hanson," James said.

His father argued. "No. No doctor."

The man was like that. He couldn't be reasoned with when it came to health matters—said he didn't like anyone poking around on him, fussing with him.

James moved to go, but his father caught him by the shirt.

"No doctor," he repeated.

James hesitated.

"D. . .don't need no doctor," his father whispered hoarsely.

Tugging the quilts over the man's chest, James warned, "If you're not better by tomorrow, I'm getting the doctor."

Silence answered him.

"Understand?"

His father nodded, but James wondered if the man understood at all. If he wasn't better by the next day, the doctor must be called. Right now, his father needed water. That much James knew. Fevers were common and could be dangerous if left to soar to unreasonable levels. Since his mother's death, his father hadn't been in the greatest of health. He seemed to catch most everything that went around. The man was frail to begin with, but James had never seen him this sick before.

Slipping into the kitchen, James retrieved a white porcelain cup and filled it with water from the pump. He retraced his steps to the bedroom and lifted his father's head off the pillow. James let the fluid trickle into his father's mouth, noting that his lips were cracked and peeling. His father drank every drop, satisfying James for the moment.

When he let the man's head down, James saw he shivered. He touched his father's whiskered cheek. "Are you cold?" he asked, knowing the fever was extremely high. Guilt twisted his insides. He really should get the doctor.

On the other hand, if his father felt well in the morning, he would be upset with him for making such a fuss. *Maybe I'm overreacting,* James thought. Suddenly his father jerked in his sleep and the shivering came on that much stronger.

James added another quilt to the two that already covered his father and waited to see if that might warm him. Still, the old man trembled convulsively.

Slowly, James slipped off his boots. He removed his gray cotton shirt and draped it across his mother's Saratoga trunk resting by the foot of the bed.

Lifting the load of blankets, James crawled into the bed and worked his way to his father's side. He tucked himself in beside his father's quaking form and wrapped strong, muscular arms around him. Sleep would not come this night.

Martha, no doubt, had imbibed in the corn liquor, probably becoming drunk. She was drinking strong liquor more often lately, losing herself in it and growing irrational when he pressed her about his concerns for her welfare. James knew he didn't love Martha. He cared for her as a friend, but he didn't love her.

For one brief moment, a prayer found its way to his lips. "Lord, I know I've not always been the person You'd have me be, and I'm truly sorry for that. Nor have I prayed much. I'm sorry for that, too. Sometimes I don't think I know how to talk to You. I'm asking something of You now, though. I'm asking for my pa. He's sick, as You can see. Take care of him for me." James never closed his eyes. The night dragged on.

three

Katelyn woke to numbness in her right leg and left arm from holding Carrie all night.

Sunlight streamed into the window, wrapping them both in its warmth. What a beautiful spring day it would be! For a brief second, Katelyn felt peace. She glanced down at her sister, alarm replacing the strange, welcome calm. Was Carrie just sleeping? Or was she. . .?

Shaking her gently, Katelyn's pulse quickened when the child wouldn't respond, wouldn't open her eyes. "No, Father in heaven," Katelyn whispered into the air. "I can't do this again."

When she heard the delicate wisp of breath ease past the little girl's pale lips, she settled back into the rocker, relieved. Then a sudden chill flooded her, and she threw her gaze in the direction of the bed. She could see the rise and fall of life beneath the blankets. Her mother had also made it through the night. Did that mean. . . ?

"No," Katelyn warned herself. She couldn't allow hope to invade her heart. Hadn't she hoped before with each member of her family? And hadn't two died with that hope? No. Not again.

Lifting the four-year-old in her arms, she rose painfully from her sitting position. She placed Carrie back in the bed, beside her mother, and covered them liberally with quilts. Then Katelyn touched a hand to each forehead. Still hot. She made a quick trip to the well.

After bathing them with cool, wet cloths, Katelyn quenched her thirst with the fresh water. Next, she began struggling out of her soiled, wrinkled clothes. It had been over a week since she'd changed or bathed. She couldn't stand the feeling any longer. Suddenly Carrie screamed.

24

Slowly Katelyn lifted the worn, filthy brown calico back up and over her slender shoulders. After checking on Carrie, she trudged out to the dugout, retrieved some sassafras root bark, and spent the next hour boiling it into a tea.

Katelyn sipped some of the brew first, allowing a portion to cool before feeding it to her sick loved ones. She had to take precautions to preserve her own health.

Labeled as a panacea of all ills, sassafras tea was Katelyn's last hope, or at least that's how she felt. She sometimes wondered why she hadn't fallen ill with the sickness, but so far she hadn't come up with any explanation.

What would the day bring? She dreaded the thought of moving a single muscle for the next twelve hours. When she stood, her legs trembled.

"I am so weak, Lord. Give me strength."

I can do all things through Christ who strengthens me. Philippians 4:13 flowed through her mind effortlessly.

"Okay, Lord, You're in charge."

Katelyn staggered to the yard, where she filled several buckets with water from the well and brought them back into the house. She boiled the water in the large, black iron kettle hanging from a pivoting crane over the fireplace. The fire warmed the cool soddie near where it blazed.

Next Katelyn created a pallet from a buffalo hide and several blankets, placing it near the hearth. She lifted Carrie from the bed and placed her fevered, shivering form onto it. She covered her with the blankets and then spread a quilt on top.

Noticing the Jacob's Ladder pattern of the quilt, Katelyn sighed. Would her younger sister soon be stepping from this world to the next, just like the angels in Jacob's dream? "How much more can you take, Carrie?" Katelyn questioned, not expecting an answer. "How much more?" She stroked her sister's blond hair away from closed eyes and studied the eruptions on the child's pretty face.

Blood oozed from them, along with yellow pus that dried in crusts around the spots. She knew the lesions made Carrie uncomfortable, yet Katelyn wondered how she might keep her sister from clawing at them in her sleep.

After the last of the water had heated, Katelyn poured it into the round tin tub, usually reserved for the household laundry. Removing her clothing, she stepped into the bathing vessel. With lye soap in hand, she scrubbed her body and washed her long chestnut-brown hair until it squeaked when she eased the water from it with her fingers.

Some of the tension in her muscles seemed to drain from her, like the dirt falling off her skin that clouded the water. She resisted stepping out, knowing what the day held in store. The rest she got, even in a chair, helped take the edge off the exhaustion she had felt for days. Carrie squirmed and moaned on the pallet in front of the strong fire, and Katelyn doused herself with one more bucket of water, this time cold.

Brushing her wet hair, Katelyn stepped into one of her mother's fresh percale dresses, a faded blue. She had no more clean items of her own. Today, she would need to wash bedding, towels, and clothes and somehow make the place more presentable.

Fully dressed, Katelyn moved into the kitchen lean-to and made warm poultices from starch paste. These she applied to Carrie's eruptions. They seemed to soothe her, for the little girl settled back into sleep. Katelyn wondered if Carrie could eat anything, but decided against trying to feed her for the moment. Later, maybe. Next she moved to her mother's side and applied the paste to the woman's sores.

Just as she stepped away from the bed, a voice spoke.

"I smell sassafras tea, Daughter."

She trembled. "Mama?"

Her mother's voice rang weak, but her words were lucid. "Drink sassafras in March, and you won't need a doctor all year."

"Yes, Mama, I know."

"Let's give another cup to Carrie, and then I want you to tell me all you know of sassafras."

Katelyn knew her mother was trying to take her mind off her situation. It worked. She nodded approval, tears brimming her long lashes. Hope had returned. And she vowed to fight with all her might to hold onto it.

Carrie coughed and cried as Katelyn forced more tea down her throat. Their mother lifted her head higher on the pillow and watched. Katelyn saw tears fill Mama's tired eyes.

"Now, tell me," Mama whispered.

Katelyn stepped to her mother's bedside and perched herself on the edge. Clearing her throat, she began.

"Sassafras was one of the first woods exported to England and was guaranteed to cure, let's see—guotidian and tertian agues, lung fevers, dropsy, liver problems, stomach ulcers, skin troubles. . .uh. . ."

"Sore eyes, catarrh, dysentery, gout," her mother offered. "It's a blood purifier and tonic and a sweater-outer of fevers—"

Katelyn picked up the dialogue. "With goldenseal and wild cherry, it makes a very potent tonic." Tears ran freely down her cheeks. "Are you okay now, Mama?"

"Yes. Yes, I think I am."

Carrie cried softly to herself.

"She needs more fluids in her," said Mama. "But first, help me to the rocker. I need to be out of this bed for a spell."

Her mother was a small woman, but her weight on Katelyn's shoulders felt immense. The combination of exhaustion and relief brought on a certain sluggish feeling. After her mother was secured in the rocker and covered by a lap blanket, Katelyn forced more water into Carrie's mouth. Still, the girl fought. Mama talked to her youngest daughter in consoling tones as she lay on the pallet near the hearth. Carrie seemed to settle down some and rested. The little girl would need to be placed back into bed soon, back into the warmth of the feather ticking and heavy blankets, but Katelyn had to wash them first. They were wet and sticky with fever and sickness.

It was still early morning when Katelyn set the washed

feathers in the garret to dry, just inside the lean-to where the sun could reach them. The bedding and other laundry dried in the sunshine on the line.

After washing down the sparse furnishings in the soddie and sweeping the puncheon floor, Katelyn cooked a pot of mush. She thinned it out with extra water and sweetened it lightly with molasses. Carrie and Abigail needed sustenance. Now. The pudding made earlier had hardened on the top. It had been two days since they'd had any food. Sallow complexions gave testimony to that fact.

Lifting the child into Mama's lap, Katelyn watched as Mama held Carrie's frail body for a moment, hugging her close. She ached for her sister, realized she would miss her so much when she joined the others. It was difficult to imagine little Carrie could possibly come through this ordeal.

The thought stirred emotions Katelyn didn't want awakened. She was tired of the sorrow, raw from it. Yet that familiar concern edged through the shadows of her mind: When would she get the sickness? Who would take care of *her?* Mama was frail from her ordeal and couldn't possibly stand up to the rigors and demands of caring for Katelyn if she fell ill.

Forcing the thought from her mind, she allowed Mama to spoon-feed Carrie as much of the mush as the child could handle. This time, Carrie accepted the nourishment. She drank some cool water as well, without struggling. Mama ate as much as she could, obviously having no appetite.

Wiping Carrie's mouth, Katelyn lifted her from Mama's lap and transferred her back onto the pallet. She noted the child wasn't as limp as before. Touching the backs of her fingers to Carrie's forehead, Katelyn noted the fever was nearly gone. When she peered into Carrie's eyes, somebody peered back. *Can this be happening?*

"Carrie? Are you awake? Can you see me?"

"Uh huh," came the hoarse reply.

Katelyn gripped her around the shoulders and held her

close, smoothing tendrils of the child's hair in a soothing gesture. She closed her eyes and breathed of her scent, so sweet and innocent. "Are you gonna be okay?"

"I want Mama," Carrie pleaded.

"Shh, Mama's real busy right now." She held her tightly, not wanting to let go. Her chin quivered.

Carrie never answered. She had fallen fast asleep. Katelyn held her sister while a tiny smile stretched her trembling lips. Hope.

James jerked awake. It took him a moment to figure out his whereabouts. He peered down at his father, who still shivered uncontrollably. That was what woke him.

A frown tugged the corners of James's lips down, and his eyebrows slanted in toward the bridge of his nose. *What are those spots all over your face?* he wanted to ask. He sat up and rolled Isaac onto his back. Working the collar of the man's long underwear back and down off his shoulders, he noticed more spots along his arms and hands, legs and feet, nearly everywhere he looked!

James's heart sank. Smallpox. Had to be. He checked his father's fever. His skin was still very hot. James rolled out of bed with effort, feeling as though he had just been punched in the stomach. How many survived smallpox? Not many—he knew that much. And his father was an old man in extremely frail health to begin with.

Struggling into his jeans and a clean muslin shirt, James slipped on his boots. He'd fetch the doctor before opening the store. Maybe the store would remain closed for the day, maybe longer. It didn't matter.

After giving his father fresh water to drink, James stoked the fire and covered the older man with plenty of blankets. Pa's eyes looked glassy, dazed, when James peered into them to tell him where he was going.

Quietly, James made his way out through the house and store and hiked down the road on foot until he arrived at the doctor's office. Doc Hanson was just heading out the door when James lifted a fist to knock.

"What brings you out this morning?" Doc Hanson asked.

Something was wrong. James could see it on the doctor's face. "My father's sick, really sick."

Doc Hanson dropped his gray gaze to the ground, then peered back at James. "Does he have the spots?"

James nodded.

"I've had three reports since last night. Another case this morning, just before you. You're the fifth." The doctor's grip tightened around the handle of his black bag, making his knuckles turn white.

"Is it smallpox?" James asked, already knowing the answer.

"Yes, son, 'fraid it is. And it's spreading like a dry prairie-grass fire."

"Can you come see my father?"

"Soon as I tend to these other folks." He paused. "Listen, son, can you do me a favor?"

"Sure. . .if I can." James worried about leaving his father unattended for too long.

"There's some folk outside of town—the Fontannas and, let me see, the McKnights." Doc rubbed at his receding hairline. "I don't know if they've been exposed, but we need to check on them. I need somebody to take a ride out, see if they're all right."

"But, my father—"

"If you'll head on out, I'll get to your father first and make sure he's being looked after."

James nodded. The doctor patted him on the back.

"Don't you worry none, son," he said. "Everything's gonna be just fine."

Everything's gonna be just fine, James repeated to himself, needing to believe that with all his heart. Without a word, James turned to go. He heard the doctor hitch his donkey to the buggy and set out to the mercantile and to the house at the back, where James's father rested.

After reaching the stables, James saddled his paint, thrust the snaffle bit into the horse's mouth, and secured the harness. He climbed onto the animal's back. Deciding he would check the Fontanna's homestead first and then the McKnights', he set out.

Two miles later, he approached the old soddie at a slow trot. It was already midmorning, but there wasn't a soul in sight. Surely somebody would be awake. Were they all still sleeping? An entire family of eight? A thumping came from the rickety barn built a good distance from the home itself. A smile lit James's face.

Tethering his pony to a thicket by the barn, James meandered into the stalls. Dismay replaced his delight. The thumping came from two aged mules kicking the walls, obviously trying to get somebody's attention. He studied them for a moment, then realized they were starving. Ribs showed through thick gray fur.

Quickly James sought out the grain sack and some stored hay. He filled two buckets with water from the pump. After feeding and watering the mules, he marched straight to the Fontanna's front door.

Without hesitation, James knocked. After a brief period, he knocked again, louder, almost banging. Then he noticed the smell: a sickeningly pungent odor coming through the cracks in the wood-plank door.

Wrinkling his nose, James turned the latch. The door swung open on rusty hinges, squeaking loudly. The horrid stench assaulted his nostrils, and he backed up two steps as though someone had shoved him.

Breathing shallowly, James pushed forward, fearful of what he knew he would find. The sight brought tears to his eyes.

Bodies lay everywhere. Some lay on mattresses of straw, others on the only double bed in the place. Two rested on the floor where they had obviously breathed their last. All eight members of the Fontanna family had been struck down by the disease! James knew he had to check each of them for some sign of life. He couldn't leave them without knowing.

His insides crawled as he made his way to each body. Tears ran down his face as he checked the final family members for signs of life. He counted to be sure he had everybody and was surprised to have only counted seven members. Weren't there eight?

He searched the room again. Nothing. He counted a second time, a third. *Who's missing?*

"Hello!" he called out. When nobody answered, he yelled a second time. "I'm here to help you!"

Something moved. He swung around, unsure. A little boy, probably six, stumbled warily from his hiding place beneath the bed. Large, fear-filled brown eyes peered up at James. The child stood beside the bed, holding a toy soldier, its red paint chipped and faded from play.

Studying him, James saw there was not a sign of smallpox on him. "Come here," he soothed. "I'm going to help you."

The child held his ground. James stepped to him and lifted the survivor to his waist. "We have to get you outta here." He carried the boy out of the house and seated him on James's horse.

The little boy rode in front of James. Neither said a word as they covered the span to the McKnight land. Bile rose in James's mouth when he saw the marked graves, both relatively fresh.

He glanced from them to the soddie and again saw no sign of life, although clothes hung from a line. Had the one who dug these graves perished as well? Would he find more dead bodies inside?

James lifted the boy to the ground, then dismounted himself. He tied the reins to the railing that surrounded the front porch and made the boy sit on the edge of one step.

"You stay here," he nearly whispered. "I'll be right back. Stay here."

His first response after approaching the door was to test

his sense of smell. If there was death inside, he would know. To his relief, he detected no hint of the hideous scent. Then he checked his optimism. The final family member could have recently passed on.

Drawing a deep breath, James lifted his fist and thumped the door soundly. No answer. He knocked again, feeling the hair on the back of his neck rise.

This time, he heard a clunk, like a dish being set down. There was movement on the other side of the door. Somebody stood there. What would he see? In what condition would he find the other person?

Slowly the door edged open, just a crack. James saw eyes peering out like large green liquid pools of fear. They were filled with an anguish James couldn't begin to measure.

"Ma'am," he said, tipping his hat. "You okay?"

The door creaked farther open, and James immediately recognized the young woman standing in front of him. He knew her name was Katelyn, one of the McKnight sisters, but that was all. He was relieved to see there were no spots on her smooth skin. But she was pale, very pale. Dark circles looped beneath her eyes.

"I–I need a doctor," she told him.

James felt his heart melt at the sound of her voice, the fear in it, the trauma that had weakened it.

He remembered the graves. "I'm sorry 'bout your family," he told her somewhat uneasily. "Seems the smallpox is spreading. My father has it, too."

Katelyn nodded but didn't invite him in.

"Is it just you left, ma'am?" he asked, needing the information to take back to the doctor.

This time Katelyn moved aside. "Come in," she offered. "It's just me, my mother, and my baby sister."

Entering the dwelling, James breathed in the freshness of the area, like somebody had recently cleaned. He glanced to a place by the hearth and saw where she had been sewing freshly washed feathers back into clean muslin. He caught sight of movement on a makeshift pallet beside the warm fire. A woman sat in a rocker nearby.

Nodding in that direction, James asked, "Is that your sister? Your mother?"

"Can you bring the doctor?" Katelyn queried, not answering his questions. "As soon as possible?"

It was then the door opened, seemingly of its own accord. The boy entered, a look of hopelessness showing on his small, dirt-smudged face.

"Toby!" Katelyn exclaimed. "What are you doing here?"

James felt relieved to discover they knew each other. He hadn't known the boy's name. When Toby didn't answer, James spoke for him, unsure of how Katelyn would handle the news.

"He's all that's left of the Fontanna family."

He saw her bottom lip quiver, and his heart ached for her again. James felt an irresistible urge to reach out, pull her to him, and hold her tight. He couldn't. They hardly knew each other.

His heart warmed when Katelyn stretched her arms out to Toby and welcomed him to her. Of course she would understand his pain—all too well. How different she was from Martha, he thought. How very different. Why hadn't he ever noticed before?

"He could stay here," Katelyn suggested, her arms wrapped around the little boy.

Relief flooded through James. He didn't know what he would do with the child. The poor boy had already seen enough death to last a lifetime. Katelyn could provide everything he might need.

"Yes," said James. "That would be good, until we find his next of kin." No telling how long that might take. "The Fontannas were a quiet family, kept to themselves mostly," he added. Nobody knew much about them.

When Katelyn didn't respond, James added, "I'll bring the doctor soon as I can." He hadn't planned on accompanying the doctor, but the words flowed out so effortlessly. He *wanted* to return.

Katelyn nodded and released Toby. She stepped to the door that still stood ajar. "Please," she implored, "as soon as possible." She allowed her gaze to drift to where her baby sister lay sleeping. "Please hurry."

"I'll bring him," he said. "Is there anything you need before I leave?"

For a moment, Katelyn said nothing. Fresh tears rose in her eyes. "Could. . .could you pile rocks on the graves?" She dropped her gaze to the floor. A tiny hiccup rose in her chest.

James nodded and reached to grip her hand. He marveled at its smallness. "I'll get it done right away," he told her, understanding her need completely. "Be strong," he added, "I'm gonna bring help."

With that, he released her fingers and set to his task. Once completed, he retrieved his horse, mounted, and rode back to town. He couldn't get Katelyn out of his mind. The feelings she stirred unnerved him.

four

When James returned, the doctor held his father's head against his own chest. "I'm sorry, son. Don't think he's going to make it."

James rushed to his father's side. The older man peered at him through glassy eyes. He whispered words, but James couldn't quite understand what the man said.

"I think he's trying to tell you something," Doc Hanson said.

Leaning closer, to where he could feel his father's hot breath against his face, James asked, "What, Father? What is it?"

"You. . .promise. . ." The voice was barely a whisper.

"Promise?" James responded. "Anything, Father, anything."

"M. . .marry the Appleburg g. . .girl."

Did I hear you right? "Marry Martha?" James's eyes widened, alarm flashing in their depths.

"Do the right. . .right thing." His father paused to draw in a shallow breath that made his whole body shake.

The old man struggled to speak again, as though every breath was fused with intense pain. "P–promise me. . . James."

He watched his father's eyelids flutter. Time was running out. His heart thumped hard and fast, making James struggle with his own breathing.

"Yes," James stated evenly. "I'll marry the Appleburg girl." The words caught in his throat like a lodged chicken bone. He felt the blood drain from his face.

The older man's eyes closed. His chest stopped its rhythmic rise and fall. He lay perfectly still.

Doc Hanson let the man's head down gently. Then he gripped the quilt and tugged it over the dead man's face.

"I'm sorry, son," the doctor said, rising to stand beside the bed. "He just couldn't fight any longer."

Feeling as though his world had collapsed, James stood, turned, and trudged from the room. He wasn't sure what he would do next. Everything around him seemed to move in slow motion, including himself.

Approaching the door to the store that separated the mercantile from the house, James barely turned the knob to open it. All his strength drained away. His grip felt weak, clammy. He found it difficult to breathe. Even the voice that rang in his ears carried an eerie echo with it.

"James?"

The voice sounded familiar, but James couldn't peg it. He felt like he should know it, but didn't, quite.

"James, help me!"

A woman. The voice belonged to a woman. Who? He glanced up, his head feeling like it weighed as much as a cannon ball. A kink formed in his neck.

"Martha," he whispered. He struggled with his emotions, not wishing to break down in front of a woman, especially Martha Appleburg. What was she doing here? She rarely, if ever, ventured into the mercantile.

"James," Martha repeated. "I need to find the doctor. Do you know where he is?"

Pointing toward the door at the back of the mercantile, he said, "In there."

Just then Doc Hanson stepped out. Martha dashed to him.

"My sister and father are sick," she almost screamed. "They've got spots all over them! I need your help!"

"Smallpox," James muttered.

"What? No!"

The doctor moved to Martha's side. "Now, girl, calm down. Hysterics won't help 'tall."

It was too late. Martha fainted, hitting her head soundly on the wood plank floor.

"Get me a cold rag," the doctor ordered, bending low to

lift Martha's eyelids and study the pupils. The bun resting at the back of her head had cushioned her fall.

James obeyed the command, still feeling as though he moved at an unbelievably slow rate.

"C'mon, son, I need your help," the doctor urged, obviously sensing James wasn't doing too well.

Although James tried to quicken his pace, he couldn't. Still, he retrieved a handkerchief from one of the shelves and left the store section briefly. When he returned, having wet the cloth from the pump, Martha came to.

Doc Hanson gripped the cloth and placed it on Martha's forehead. "Breathe nice and slow for me, Martha."

Panic laced every word Martha uttered. "We can't have the smallpox! We just can't! *I* can't!"

"Shhh," Doc Hanson soothed. "Everything's going to be fine, just fine."

James felt his blood boil. Hadn't the good doctor just told him that very same thing? Right before he agreed to go check on the families living outside of town?

"How can you tell her that?" he nearly shouted. "It's not going to be fine! Everybody's coming down with this. It's an epidemic." He drew a deep breath and ran stiff fingers through his coal-black hair. "We're right in the middle of a plague. You know that. Don't pretend you don't!"

Doc Hanson didn't respond. He helped Martha to her feet. Veins stood out on his forehead, and his complexion looked unusually flushed. Martha stumbled momentarily, but he steadied her.

James stepped in closer to them. "What's wrong with you?" he asked the man. "You don't look right. Are you feeling okay?"

"Fine, fine, son. Just need to get my bearings is all."

"You sure you're okay?" James studied the doctor with a side glance, unsure of what to think.

"Yes. Can you take care of Martha while I head to the Appleburg home?"

All James could do was nod. What would he do with Martha when he hadn't had so much as a moment to absorb his father's death? He didn't feel like he had the energy to deal with anybody else's problems yet—least of all with Martha's.

As though reading James's thoughts, the doctor added, "It'll keep your mind on other things." He walked to where James stood, leaving Martha to grip the counter to hold herself upright. "I'm sorry, James. Wish this weren't happening, but I'm gonna need your help. Can you help me?"

Again, James nodded. Doc Hanson patted him on the back.

James thought he saw a tear slip from one of the doctor's round gray eyes.

"You sure you're okay?" James asked again.

"Wife's taken ill," said Doc Hanson, dabbing the tear with his index finger and tugging his long black duster tighter around himself, as though chilled. "Need to get my bag," he added. "Left it in the other room."

"I'll get it," James offered.

"No, no," the man argued. "You don't need to be going back there right now. Just help Martha. I've got to finish my rounds, make arrangements for those who have passed on."

Within seconds Doc Hanson retrieved his bag and left the store. James heard the clanking of chains and the thud of horse hooves pounding the dirt as the doctor rode away. He turned his attention to Martha. Yet, when he peered at her, his mind filled with images of Katelyn. Confused, he shook his head, trying to clear his thoughts.

Stepping to Martha, James gripped her beneath one arm and moved her to a nearby flour barrel.

"Here," he said, "Have a seat." When she had, he asked, "Tell me what happened."

Martha began to cry. Her cries went from mild tones to near screaming.

James had no words of comfort to offer. *I'm not telling her everything's going to be fine,* he thought, remembering the doctor's words as though they had been burned into his mind with a hot branding iron. *Can't offer hope if there's none to be had.* He let her cry until she seemed spent of tears.

All of Martha's rouge disappeared, and the bodice of her purple silk dress darkened from the tears falling off her trembling chin.

"Now," he said, "can you talk?"

"My family is contagious," she gushed, "and I'm going to catch the smallpox, James. I know I am."

"You don't know that for certain," James admonished, her words striking him in an odd way. *Why is she worried for herself only?* he wondered.

"I can't die, James, I just can't." She cried harder.

Turning his head from side to side to alleviate the kink in his neck, he told her, "You're not going to die, Martha. You have to get hold of yourself!"

He chastised himself inwardly for being too hard on her. "I'm sorry, Martha, it's just that we need to tend the sick. We have to do something to help Doc Hanson." He felt stronger just from hearing his own words. "We have to help the doctor."

Martha didn't seem to be listening. She peered at James as though he'd gone crazy. "I–I just don't have the strength to tend the sick, James," she mumbled.

"We have to, Martha. Don't you see that?"

Nothing.

"Martha, we must help the doctor. He needs our help."

Suddenly Martha stood. She wiped away residual tears with the back of a gloved hand. "Then you do it, James!" she screamed. "I can't be around the sick! What if they give it to me?"

Her words came fast. "Aren't we. . .uh. . .supposed to quarantine them?" she asked. "I've heard of that. Haven't you?"

James could only stare at her with disbelief.

"These sick people need to be away from us healthy ones—"

"Martha," James interrupted, "settle down." Then he said the words he didn't want to say. "Everything will be just fine."

ða

Carrie asked for a drink. Katelyn felt her shoulders relax. She smiled as she moved to where her baby sister lay on the bed. Her mother lay beside the child, sleeping.

"What would you like?" Katelyn asked, barely able to suppress her joy.

"Wadda."

"Good. That's very good. I'll go get you some water."

As she dipped the ladle into the water bucket, Katelyn felt a new source of energy rise within her. It was as though she had slept eight hours to awaken to a beautiful sunrise. She even forgot she'd asked for the doctor only hours earlier. Now, she remembered. She also remembered James—how kind he was with eyes full of compassion.

With the worry over whether her remaining loved ones would survive nearly gone, she couldn't keep images from rising in her mind, images of James. Katelyn allowed them to take form however they chose. This only added to her energy level. Would he return? With the doctor? Or, would she not see him again?

"Huwwy," said the soft voice behind her.

Carrie. I almost forgot about you! Katelyn's steps quickened with a new lightness as she closed the distance to her sister. She handed the ladle to Carrie, who gripped it in both hands and placed it against her pale lips. The child took liberal swallows before handing the empty ladle back to Katelyn.

Katelyn let it rest in her lap. "How do you feel, baby?" she asked, her words charged with hope.

"My bug bites itch," Carrie complained.

A giggle rose in Katelyn's chest. "Well, don't scratch the bug bites," she warned gently, "or they won't stop itching."

"Awwight," Carrie agreed, squirming beneath the blankets and quilts. "It's hot in here," she added.

Katelyn returned the ladle to the bucket. At Carrie's side, she gripped the blankets that covered the child. "Here," she offered, "let's get these off you." She drew them downward, but tucked them in beside her mother so the woman wouldn't get chilled. Slight fevers still plagued both patients.

A voice behind her caused her to turn her head in anticipation. It was Toby Fontanna. The child had asked to go outside to play in the dirt just after James left. Katelyn checked on him periodically to be sure he was all right. She was worried about how he was feeling after having lost his entire family and thought that letting the boy play might allow him to momentarily escape the pain of what he had just endured.

"I'm hungry, ma'am," he said, matter-of-factly.

The boy was six, give or take a few months, but he seemed so grown-up. Katelyn didn't remember him being like that, and she had known Tobias Jobe Fontanna since his birth. There was a strange new tone in his voice that had a grown-up quality to it, even though he still sounded like a boy. She glanced back at Carrie.

"Can I get Toby something to eat?" she asked.

"Me, too," was Carrie's reply, nodding vigorously.

Katelyn stood. "I've got some mush left. I can sweeten it with molasses. Would you like that?"

Both children nodded in unison. Katelyn moved to the cupboard and retrieved two tin plates. She dipped into the larger bowl of mush with a wooden spoon and allowed several dollops to drop into each tin. Next, she filled two tumblers with fresh water. Having set two places at the table, she called for Toby.

He dashed to his place as though starving.

"Poor thing." Katelyn rubbed his head of scruffy brown hair and made a mental note to give him a bath soon.

Next, she stepped to the bedside and lifted Carrie in her arms, attempting to tote the little girl to her place at the table. Her baby sister would have none of it.

"I want to walk," she said, nearly wriggling from Katelyn's grasp.

"Are you sure?"

Carrie never answered, so Katelyn set her on her slipper-clad feet. For a moment, the child merely stood, seeming as though she might tumble over at any minute.

"The woom is moving," she said at last.

"Moving? What do you mean?"

"It looks funny," Carrie tried to explain.

"Vertigo," said Katelyn. "You're just weak is all. Once you have something good in your tummy, you should feel much better." She paused. "Want me to carry you?"

When the little girl raised her arms upward, Katelyn scooped her up, stepped to the pine trestle table, and set her down in front of her plate of food. Toby had already devoured his mush and was attempting to transfer more out of the bowl into his tin plate. Once she had them settled, she stepped back to the bed where her mother slept.

"Mama?" she whispered, eager for her mother to see Carrie up and about. "Wake up."

The woman stirred, moaned, then opened her eyes. "Mornin'," she managed.

"Look," said Katelyn, pointing toward the two children eating a short distance from them.

Turning her head ever so slightly, her mother's face broke into a smile. "Carrie," she whispered. "The baby's gonna be fine." As though the news calmed her, she slipped back into sleep.

"Yeah, Mama, Carrie's gonna be fine." Katelyn glanced upward. "We're all gonna be fine now."

❧

Martha refused to leave James's side, refused to return home to assist her ailing loved ones. She had busied herself study-ing the various looking glasses and hair combs in the women's section of the store. He watched her with a growing sense of discontent.

In one way, she frustrated him; in another, he felt incredi-bly sorry for her. It seemed to him, she tried to forget what was happening around them, even hummed as she moved to study the bolts of cloth that had recently arrived with a shipment of canned goods.

His attention was diverted as a person entered the mercantile. John Dorman, a good friend who ran the livery stable, approached James.

"I need some food," John said, without preamble.

James sensed a certain weariness in the man. "How's the family?" he asked, retrieving a cloth sack from behind the counter. Martha continued to hum contentedly as she browsed.

John's whiskered chin trembled ever so slightly, but he bucked off his emotions. "Wife's okay," he offered, "but I lost two o' my chillens." He hesitated and wiped a filthy palm across his scraggly new growth of beard.

"Sorry," James offered, trying not to dwell on his own grief. He ached, but the ache wouldn't surface, couldn't with all the confusion. A certain weariness threatened to cloud his ability to reason.

He handed the sack to the man. "Get what you need."

"Can't pay ya right now," John told him. "Ain't been able to work with the family sick. Will start back today."

James shook his head. "Don't worry about that right now. Just get your groceries and tend to your kids."

John roamed the mercantile, filling the bag with cornmeal, other staples, and a few canned goods. He left without a backward glance.

Glancing in Martha's direction, James tried to figure his next move. She wasn't acting right, seemed disoriented. He rose and crossed to where she stood running her hand over a section of gingham.

"This cloth's not real comfortable against delicate skin," she said. "Silk's best."

James thought she said this more to herself than to him.

"Martha, you okay?"

Martha smiled up at him. "I'm just fine, James. And you?"

He gripped her by both shoulders and turned her around to

face him square. "You're not fine, Martha, admit it." He *had* to reach her. She was to be his wife.

Then she started to cry. He folded his arms around her trembling form and drew her to him. "Go ahead and cry."

She did. Hard. But he couldn't. Not yet.

five

Katelyn set to the task of washing dishes. Toby fell asleep on the pallet near the hearth—the one she had earlier created for Carrie—shortly after he ate.

Carrie and Mother slept, too, in the freshly washed bed. The knock at the door made Katelyn jump. She peered around the room. Nobody had woken. *Good,* she thought, *very good. They need their sleep.*

Drying her hands on the white apron tied around her waist, Katelyn moved to open the door. Excitement swelled within her when she saw James on the other side, but it died just as quickly when Martha stepped out from behind him.

Almost forgot, Katelyn mused, *James and Martha have been courting for some time now. It would be reasonable that she'd be with him.* A cold sensation filled her chest, even more so when she peered into James's eyes. She sensed something terribly wrong.

Removing his hat, James said, "Katelyn, I needed to let you know what's happening in town."

"Did you bring the doctor?" Katelyn asked.

"That's why I'm here."

Martha interrupted the dialogue. "The doctor's at my place right now. He may not even get to you for a while."

James rubbed his left temple and gripped his Stetson in one hand. "Seems we've got an epidemic," he continued. "The doctor's doin' the best he can to get to all the folks who need him, but. . ."

Managing a slight smile, Katelyn informed him, "It's all right. My mother and baby sister took a turn for the better. By the grace of God," she added.

Peering at the ground, James asked, "May we come in?"

At his question, Martha stumbled backward, as though something frightened her. "I'm not going in there if her family has that nasty disease! And you'd better not either, James!"

He turned to look back at Martha, his brows furrowed. "You can stay out here if you wish, but I need to talk with Katelyn." James swiped at a section of porch with his hat to remove excess dirt. "Sit down here, 'til I come out to get you."

Martha obeyed, and James stepped inside. Katelyn closed the door.

"They're all sleeping," she explained, moving her right hand through the air as though the act might better convey her meaning. "And they're doing better. I prayed, James, and they're doing better."

James didn't know what hand God had in this whole mess, but hadn't he prayed, too? And, his father had died despite his prayers.

Katelyn caught the shadow crossing his dark brown eyes. "Are you okay?" she asked.

"My father passed away a few hours ago." He paused. "I also think something's wrong with the doctor."

"I'm so sorry," Katelyn offered. Her heart ached for him, knowing firsthand what such a loss felt like. She had to work hard to keep tears at bay. And what had James just said about the doctor?

"Don't know for sure what's wrong with the doctor," said James, answering her unspoken question. "He doesn't look right."

Stepping to the pine table, Katelyn sat down. "I hope he's not coming down with the smallpox," she stated. "What will we do if he does?"

Taking a seat beside her, James set his black Stetson on the table. "How's your mother doing?"

"I think she's going to be all right. Carrie, too."

"Good. Do you think your mother's strong enough to assist the doctor?"

Katelyn's lips pursed in thought. "I don't know, James. I don't think she can do much of anything at this time. The illness left her in a weakened state. I'm not sure how long it'll be before she regains her strength."

"Hmm," James mumbled. "Doc Hanson really needs some help. He can't possibly handle this whole affair on his own. He needs somebody else with knowledge of medicine and treatments and such. Your mom, Abigail, is good at that sort of thing."

A sense of pride rose up inside Katelyn. Yes, her mother was very good at what she did. Problem was, she was incapable of handling anything rigorous at the moment. She peered at James. He seemed to be studying the floor as though answers to his thoughts were written there.

How handsome he was, Katelyn decided, taking the opportunity to look him over. His black hair shone with blue highlights when the sun hit it just right, it was so dark. And the rich black lashes framing his chocolate brown eyes gave them a slightly sleepy look although he was wide awake. Full lips were as finely chiseled as his strong bone structure. She glanced down at his hands.

Tanned, they had a certain masculine quality to them that stood out due to his long fingers. Everything about him seemed perfect. Katelyn felt something stir within her and dropped her gaze immediately. Why hadn't she noticed him before? she wondered.

"I can help," she offered.

He looked at her, head tilted in obvious puzzlement. "You?"

She didn't quite know how to explain it to him, so she just plunged in, hoping for the best. "I have my mother's gift of healing," she explained. "I've watched her for years, and I've learned a lot. Of course, I have much, much more to learn."

James sat straight up in his seat. "Would you be able to do this?"

"Guess I have to, James." She pulled her bottom lip between

her teeth, pondering her new role. "My mother's frail, yes, but her mind is keen. Should I have questions, she can still assist."

"But are you sure you're up to the task. The epidemic is attacking with a fury I've never seen before. And what if the doctor—"

"James," hastened Katelyn, "the Lord will not give us more than we can handle. If Doc Hanson becomes ill, then we'll take care of him, too."

"We?"

"That's right."

"I don't know how to tend the sick, Katelyn."

A half grin played against Katelyn's lips. "I don't mean you'll have to tend the sick, so to speak. I may need help with the stout patients. But I'll direct all that. What you can oversee is the heavy work." She pointed at the cupboards and continued.

"You own the town mercantile. Folks will be needing food, supplies, and medicines. Also I'm going to need some cots made to serve as beds. You've got bolts of durable cloth at the mercantile, don't you?"

"Plenty."

"We just have to organize." She paused. "Is the doctor suggesting a quarantine site?"

"Don't know," James answered. "He's just trying to get around to all his patients. I'm sure he's thought of it."

Again, Katelyn forced her bottom lip between her teeth, in deep thought. "I think we should consider the Fontanna homestead as the quarantine site. We can use my home if necessary, but I'll have to have assistance as I can't be two places at once."

"I'll take that to Doc Hanson," said James. "See what he thinks."

"Good, and I'll talk with Mother. I'm sure she'd agree."

Rising, James retrieved his hat from the table and held it. "The sooner we get things moving, the better. Things are getting worse in town."

"And it may continually worsen for some time."

Nodding, James said, "Thanks for your help, Katelyn. I really appreciate this."

"It's just something we must do, James. No thanks are needed."

He made his way to the front door.

Katelyn watched as he opened it. For some reason she didn't want him to go. She wanted him to stay, forever. When she saw Martha outside on the step, her heart sank. How could this be? She had not been attracted like this to anybody before, and he was already in love with somebody else.

James and Martha made their departure. Katelyn went to the hearth and sat down in the slat-backed rocker. She had time to think while everybody was asleep. Besides, free time might be very limited once Doc Hanson set the necessary plans in motion.

Something bothered her, though. Something she couldn't quite get out of her mind. James. And Martha.

She hadn't witnessed the type of attraction between the two that normally could be sensed when a young couple was on the brink of a lifetime together. Their relationship seemed strained. He acted short on patience with her, and she with him.

Katelyn let her eyes rest on Toby, but she didn't see him. *Maybe it's due to the loss of loved ones and all the agony that goes with it.* Yes, that had to be it. Still, the situation troubled her.

As far as Katelyn was concerned, Martha didn't seem James's type. He was much more serious, thoughtful. Martha was too preoccupied with herself—not at all concerned with those around her. They were as different as day and night.

Chewing on her bottom lip, Katelyn resigned herself to the fact that she didn't have all the answers. Besides, who was she to judge who was right for whom?

Stifling a yawn, Katelyn allowed her eyes to close. She didn't realize how tired she was. Nor did she know how little time there would be for rest in the days to come.

❧

When James returned to the mercantile, his father's body had already been removed. A note left on the pillow instructed James to be at the cemetery by sunset. That's when his father would be buried along with the others who had already passed away. They would need James's help with the digging.

"Martha, I need to take you home," James stated.

Crossing her arms firmly in front of her, Martha answered, "I'm not going back to that place. Maggie's ill, Father's ill, and one of the servants. I think Mother's getting the nasty stuff, too. I'm not going back!"

"Yes, you are," James said succinctly. "You've already been exposed," he added. "Additional exposure won't make a difference one way or another."

Martha started to cry.

James waited. "You could make the situation better by tending to your family. They need your help, Martha."

Rubbing at her swollen eyes, Martha said, "I just can't, James. I can't."

"Well, that's fine. But I'm still taking you home. You can stay outside if need be, but I have to be sure you're safe." He hesitated. Then he added, "I've got to bury my father and others later. Do you want to come to the cemetery with me?"

"Heavens no!" Martha's chest rose with the inhalation of a deep breath. "Be around those dead people? No!"

"Then there's only one option," James stated, making his way to Martha. "You have to go home for a while."

Martha said nothing. James thought mention of the cemetery might have something to do with it. He gripped her gently by the arm and led her outside.

"Get in your buggy, and I'll follow you on my horse. I'd like to see if I can be of assistance in some way to your family." Wrapping both hands around her waist, James lifted Martha into the carriage and handed her the reins. She took off, leaving a trail of white dust.

Next, he untied his horse from the post at the front of the

store, pulled the reins over the horse's head, and mounted the animal. He followed Martha, staying a safe distance behind to avoid being swallowed up in the spray of dirt she left in her wake.

The Appleburg ranch was located on the other side of town, directly north of the McKnight homestead and the Fontanna place. It was a couple miles from town. As they approached, James admired the abundant head of longhorn cattle grazing inside a large section of land surrounded by barbed wire fencing.

A two-story Victorian home graced the property. It struck James as awkward. The home didn't match the landscape. Although beautifully constructed, it simply didn't mesh with the roughness of its surroundings. The barn, completed recently, was the only building on the land that stood a chance of fitting in with the frontier wilderness surrounding it.

James remembered the lumber Gabe Appleburg had transported in from the East, first to build the home, then the new barn. The old barn was torn down and some of its lumber used for the current version.

Pulling up in front of the house, James warily watched Martha, who remained sitting in the carriage. At first she didn't move. James dismounted and tied his horse to a brass post at the porch that ran around the entire home. A white picket fence framed a portion of land just off to the side of the house.

Making his way to Martha's side, James helped her down from the rig. She stood stiff with reserve, viewing the house as though loathing it.

"You coming in with me?"

Martha shook her head vehemently from side to side. "No, James, I absolutely won't!"

Removing his hat as manners dictated, James made his way up the wooden steps and to the door. He lifted the brass knocker and gave three solid thumps before releasing it. Within seconds, he viewed a figure through the frosted glass oval centered on it. The door opened.

Allowed entry by the house servant, James stood in the foyer on an elliptical, hand-woven rug. The servant, a small man, gazed at James questioningly.

"Are you expected?"

Clearing his throat, James said, "No, I'm not. But, I'd like to see the gentleman of the house. If I may."

"I'll see if Mr. Appleburg is up to visitors," the servant offered. "Whom shall I say is calling?"

"James Connor."

The small man made his departure.

While he waited, James studied the surroundings. Much of the furnishings were familiar to him because they were similar to those he'd seen so often in the homes of the wealthy back East, as well as in his own home.

The servant returned. "Come this way," he told James.

James followed quietly as he was led through a series of rooms papered with panoramic landscapes and historic scenes. Eventually he came to the parlor. The servant slipped in ahead of James.

"Sir," the servant announced, "Mr. Connor is here."

"Send him in," said the raspy voice on the other side of the door.

With a slight bow, the servant faced James and opened the door wide. As soon as James stepped in, the door closed.

The scent of rich tobacco filled James's nostrils. His eyes scanned black walnut, rosewood, and mahogany furnishings on slender, cabriole legs with whorl feet. The tables featured white marble tops. The moldings around the ceiling of the room were carvings of fruit and leaves. Gabe Appleburg motioned James to sit in a chair with a balloon-shaped back.

James allowed his gaze to rest on the man positioned in an overstuffed seat opposite him. A small table holding a terra cotta vase of peacock feathers and other curios rested between them.

"I'm sorry to hear about your father," Mr. Appleburg started.

James nodded but said nothing on the subject. "How's Maggie?" he asked instead.

"Not well, James."

For a second, James studied the stocky man, his white hair unkempt, his attire wrinkled. White stubble showed on his usually fresh-shaven face. At first James thought worry might have caused this dramatic change in appearance, until he saw the red tinge in Gabe Appleburg's cheeks.

"How are you feeling, Mr. Appleburg?" James asked, certain the fever was upon the man.

"Not too well. Not many in town got vaccinated against the smallpox. My family and I are included in that number." He stared at his hands. "Most of us were traveling to Cimarron from faraway places. You never think of things like preventing smallpox."

A slight edginess rose in James, but he squelched it. He hadn't been vaccinated, either. With the move, they had decided to wait.

"Mr. Appleburg, sir, I came to bring Martha home and to inform you she's having a rather difficult time."

The man nodded understanding. "Martha's like that. I would have expected it. Where is she?"

"Outside. I brought her home, but she refuses to come in—thinks she'll get the smallpox if she's around anybody with it."

"She's already exposed," said Mr. Appleburg without looking up.

"I've told her that, but I don't think she's accepting of it."

Mr. Appleburg drew a long pull on the cigar, then squashed it out in a nearby ashtray. "I'll speak with Martha. Thank you for bringing my daughter home. I've been worried about her."

Shifting closer to the edge of his seat, James lifted one hand in the air. "There's something else I need to discuss with you, sir."

"Carry on," said the older man.

James hadn't planned on this! He'd thought he would take care of his promise to his father when things had died down.

Now with Martha's father sick. . .

"Well, Mr. Appleburg, as you know, I've been courting your daughter for more than eleven months."

"Yes, I'm aware." The man clasped a crystal goblet resting on a side table with short, stubby fingers. He took a long sip, made an airy sound as it traveled down his throat, then set the glass back in its proper place. "I'm chilled, and this seems to warm me."

James wanted to tell him to drink water, lots of it, but chose to refrain.

"Well, sir, the time has come." James felt the knot form in his throat, as though attempting to prevent the words from leaving his lips.

"Go ahead, boy, make your case."

"I–I'd like to ask for your daughter's hand in m. . .marriage."

An unsettled silence filled the room.

"Do you intend to care for her, in sickness and in health?" Gabe broke the hush.

"I do." *Those words.* "I mean, *I will* do that, sir. Of course."

The man's next question stung. "How's your little business doing by way of the dollar, boy?"

James wished the man would quit referring to him as *boy*. He was making a man's decision. Was he not?

"The mercantile is doing very well, Mr. Appleburg."

Leaning forward, the older man stared into James's eyes with cold blue eyes. "Then you would be able to give her the life to which she has grown accustomed?"

Oh, Father, why did you make me promise to do this thing? A hot sensation filled James's stomach. It suddenly occurred to him that Martha's personality and priorities were not entirely her fault. She'd been raised in a materialistic world that allowed little time for internal, spiritual growth. He felt sorry for her.

"All I can offer," he explained, "is to give Martha the best life I can. We will have good times and bad times, as is the norm, sir. If she'll accept that, and me, then I'll take her hand in marriage within the month."

Mr. Appleburg slumped back in his chair, wiping at his watery eyes. After tugging another swig from his glass, he answered. "Very well, then, you have my blessings."

James thought he should smile, do something, to show appreciation, but he couldn't. "Thank you, Mr. Appleburg. I will make your daughter happy."

Something occurred to him. "Where is Mrs. Appleburg?" he asked, hoping he wasn't asking too many questions.

"Sick," replied his future father-in-law. "Whimsy is very sick. Sent her to bed an hour ago."

As though in pain, James rose from his chair and extended his hand. The older man grasped it, and they shook hands as if sealing a deal.

"Take care, boy."

James nodded and made his exit. He wove his way through the halls and rooms to find himself back in the foyer.

"James!" a voice called.

James turned in the direction of the voice and recognized a trembling figure at the top of the stairs. Doc Hanson.

"Doc? What's wrong?"

Before the man could answer, he fell to his knees. The black bag clanked down the stairs ahead of the man, who tumbled after it like a limp doll before settling beside his bag and its scattered contents on the landing.

six

James raced to the doctor's side. A crimson red pool of blood grew beneath the older man's head. The servant, obviously hearing the crash, dashed to the foot of the stairs and knelt beside James, his face doughy white.

Panic caused the servant's voice to rise. "We must get the doctor!" He stood. "Somebody get the doctor!"

Bending low, James positioned his right cheek over the doctor's lips. No breath. The servant grew frantic by the second.

"Will somebody get the doctor?"

James turned and tugged on the servant's pant leg. Whispering, he said, "This *is* the doctor." James felt a weight of responsibility resting on his shoulders like none he had ever experienced before.

An epidemic had invaded their peaceful, prospering town and the only physician around for miles had just died. What were they to do? James sensed that before long, most of the townsfolk might respond just as the servant had: with hysteria. He had to take control.

Standing, he turned until he faced the servant. "Listen to me," he directed, "I need you to tell Mr. Appleburg what happened. I'll track the sheriff down and let him know the details."

"Yes, sir," the servant replied, obviously more content following orders than giving them.

James found his own way out, said good-bye to Martha, mounted his paint, and sped off toward town. After checking the sheriff's office and finding no one, not even a deputy, he made the rounds at local businesses. Finally he discovered the sheriff at John Dorman's livery stable. The two were chatting over a sorrel the sheriff needed to have shod.

James stole a moment to appreciate the smells of leather and horse lather, which he loved. His gaze spotted a palomino, a clayband, an albino, and several bays.

John waved at James, then started dishing out buckets of oats and tearing off sections of hay to feed the animals. Sheriff McMillan greeted James.

"Sorry ta hear 'bout yer pa, James. Sorry, indeed."

Again, James moved around the topic, not wishing to dwell on it. "Sheriff," he said, "there's been an accident at the Appleburg place. Doc Hanson took a bad fall down the stairs after treating the sick family members. He was sick, himself. Probably had more than he could take and collapsed. He's dead, I'm afraid."

The sheriff drew a deep breath and dabbed at sweat forming on the back of his neck. "Any witnesses?"

"I saw it happen."

"How?"

James informed the sheriff of that and much more. Cimarron was in trouble without a doctor. Abigail McKnight was in no shape to assume his duties. Could Katelyn possibly handle this load?

Shaking his head in obvious disbelief, the sheriff said, "I'll have one of my deputies load the body and bring it to town. Need to inform his wife. Any idea where she might be?"

"Yes," said James. "She's home in bed, sick."

Without another word, the sheriff took his leave.

James knew his next move must be to get back to Katelyn and let her know what had transpired. The town's health rested in the hands of Katelyn McKnight and her knowledge of medicinal plants and treatments. He would do whatever he could to help, knowing the next days would not be easy.

When he approached the McKnight door, James found Toby playing contentedly outside with his toy soldier.

"Hi, Mister," the boy said, peering up into the sun, which made his warm brown eyes appear translucent. Dirt streaked his face and homespuns.

He looked somehow better to James. "Hi, Mister, to you," he teased. But Toby didn't smile, didn't seem to acknowledge the attempt at humor. Instead, he went back to his make-believe world.

Shrugging his shoulders, James lifted his hat off his head, stepped to the door, and knocked. After a few seconds, the door opened.

"Come in," Katelyn beckoned. She glanced around, pleased to find Martha absent. "Where's Martha?" she asked, suddenly ashamed of her thoughts. She vowed to do better.

"She's at home right now—not doing too well."

"I understand," Katelyn obliged, not wishing to tread on privacy. "Where's the doctor? Have you talked with him yet?"

Rubbing his left temple, James motioned toward the bench at the pine table with his hat. "Can we sit down?"

"Of course." Katelyn secretly berated herself for her bad manners. *What's wrong with me?* She took her seat beside him. An unexpected shiver ran down the length of her spine. She pulled her hair off her shoulders, allowing it to run down her back where it touched her waist.

"What is it, James?" Her brows raised in arches above green eyes, creating a puzzled expression.

"I'm afraid there's been a terrible accident," he told her. "The doctor fell down a flight of stairs and is gone."

For a long moment, Katelyn didn't breathe. Time froze. "How can this be?" she finally whispered.

"I don't know."

Katelyn raised her head, gazed into James's eyes. "What do we do now?"

"You had as good a plan as any, Katelyn. I say we do what we discussed earlier. Have you talked with your mother yet?"

"No, she's still sleeping. But I'm sure there won't be a problem." She stood. "Why don't you get started on those cots, James, and see if you can clear the Fontanna homestead out? We'll need the stove, the table, cooking supplies, access to fresh water, toweling, and such. The rest of the furnishings must go so we can put beds in there."

"I'll get started after sunset, stay up all night if need be. Gabe Appleburg has some spare lumber. I'll get that to frame the cots."

"Good," said Katelyn. "I'll need to clean the Fontanna place before we start using it. Tomorrow I'll take the children with me. Mother will be fine on her own for the day."

"Anything else?"

Katelyn studied James, impressed by the way he had taken on this challenge. It only served to boost her own resolve. Somehow, she believed, with the two of them working together, they could handle anything. As this thought entered her mind, so did the guilt.

Martha. He was in love with Martha. Wasn't he? It wouldn't be right to allow these feelings to multiply and grow. She had to stop them. But how? It was almost as though she had no choice. But she did!

"Anything else?" James queried a second time.

"W. . .what? Oh, yes." Katelyn steadied her nerves, forced her mind to focus. "I'll need to have a count of all the townsfolk who have been vaccinated. We'll be needing their help."

James rose from his seat. "I'll get on it," he said. "Don't worry, Katelyn. Everything will be fine." For the first time since the epidemic had begun, he somehow believed those words. All the evidence surrounding him, however, told him otherwise.

ॐ

Carrie was up and about, playing as any healthy little girl would, with her new friend, Toby. Her face was minimally pocked. For this, Katelyn was grateful. She would most likely grow out of her scars.

Pacing the floor, Katelyn wondered what had become of James. Night came and went, but he hadn't showed. Already, it was midmorning.

"Come sit in front of me," said her mother from the rocker by the hearth.

Katelyn walked over, plopped down, and crossed her legs beneath her like a pretzel. "What, Mama?"

Her mother smoothed her nightgown with her hands, her face serious. "You have a big job ahead of you, Daughter," she stated. "Can you handle it?"

"I have to, Mama."

"That's right. And you've already done very well, organizing and such. You've taken charge, and I'm proud of you. We've had our own losses to deal with." Katelyn's mother paused, and her eyes filled with tears. "Most folk would become hysterical when faced with such adversity. You haven't."

Lowering her eyes, Katelyn thought about that for a moment. She realized she was stronger than she thought. *I can do all things through Christ who strengthens me.* The verse brought comfort time and time again. That's where she received her strength—she knew the fact without doubt. She had prayed for strength, and that prayer had been answered.

Now, she would lift up other prayers for the town. She had to rely on a faith like none other. Obstacles such as these might rock even the strongest of believers. Katelyn knew she couldn't give in. Not now. Not ever.

"I need you to listen to me," Mama said. "James will be here soon, and you'll need to start making preparations to care for the sick."

"I'll need to clean the Fontanna place," Katelyn agreed.

"And while you wait for James, you'll need to begin preparing medicines and teas." She leaned back in the rocker, allowing it to squeak. "I've got some spicebush, plenty of it, in the dugout. You'll need to brew it into a tea to induce sweating and reduce the fevers. Sassafras will also be good. If one doesn't work, try the other."

Listening intently, Katelyn nodded. "Can't I use wild pansy for the skin eruptions?"

"Yes, that should work. Grind the leaves on the metate with the mano and apply the powder to the sores. It's usually used for boils and such, but it should work fine. Also, yellow dock. The crushed leaves applied to the worst of the sores should bring about a discharge of pus. May help with the scarring. Don't know for sure, though."

"I know where everything is," Katelyn said.

"You'd best get started. We have a few cotton sacks. Have James bring you some burlap from the mercantile, since you'll be hauling the stuff back and forth. Make sure you keep plenty of this on hand."

Rising, Katelyn made a motion to leave. She knew time was of the essence. Her mother was right. Why pace and worry when things could be accomplished to aid the situation? "I'm taking Carrie and Toby with me. Will you be all right for a while?"

"I'll be just fine. I can nap in the chair or lay down on this pallet here if I need to sleep." She smiled up at Katelyn, tears brimming in her eyes. "I know you'll do well," she said confidently. "Cimarron needs you. Our time to mourn will come later."

With her mother's encouraging words in her ears, Katelyn spun on her heel and made her way out of the house and to the dugout. She retrieved the necessary herbs, including some ground ginger to help with nausea. Before long, Katelyn had two sacks of ground leaves. She would set the tea to boil when she arrived at the Fontanna homestead, after the sick were brought in. It occurred to her the Fontanna homestead would not only serve as a quarantine site, but a makeshift hospital as well. *Oh, for Cimarron to have its own hospital, like the big cities.*

She heard the knock. James! Katelyn dashed to the door, opened it without hesitation. To her dismay, Martha once again graced the porch. For a long moment Katelyn gazed at the woman, not realizing she stared. Dressed in a black riding habit of heavy silk taffeta with grosgrain lapels, she looked absolutely resplendent. Katelyn swallowed hard as though attempting to put down the envy rising up inside her.

Martha's paletot-style jacket with bell-shaped sleeves was worn over a soft batiste blouse. On the crown of her straw-brimmed hat rested a bevy of ostrich tips. A black veil attached to the hat covered her face, protecting Martha from inhaling dust thrown by horses' hooves. Kid gloves covered her hands.

Obviously, Martha had decided to enter the Appleburg home, if only to stop in her own bedroom to change clothes, Kate decided.

James entered without a word. His sudden movement diverted her attention to the things at hand. She swallowed hard again, feeling agitated with herself. *Forgive me, Lord,* she prayed silently. She studied James. He looked as though he *had* stayed up all night.

"You look tired, James," Katelyn managed to say, her bottom lip finding its usual place between her teeth.

Removing his hat, James stated, "Am tired, real tired. Stayed up all night, but got it done. The cots are already over there." He looked at the floorboards. "Buried my father, the Fontanna family, and others last night. Place is cleared out except for what you needed."

Katelyn's heart melted like tallow beneath a warm sun. He had worked so diligently, all while suffering great sorrow. A deep respect for this man took root in Katelyn. She more than liked James. She felt drawn to him somehow. His obvious compassion touched her in a way she couldn't define. *He must truly care for the people of Cimarron,* she thought, *to have worked so diligently to supply their needs while taking little concern for his own. Martha has no idea of the person she has in James.*

Katelyn felt a tear break the crest of her lower lid. If she had James's love, she would treasure it with every part of her being.

Cold filled the cavity where her heart kept a steady beat. It was obvious he was drawn to the Appleburg woman, and rightfully so. Martha was truly a beauty. She had wealth and power. What could Katelyn, herself, possibly offer a man like James? With his interests? What would he ever see in her? How life hurt!

ஃ

James studied Katelyn. Viewing her was to his eyes like fresh air to lungs that had breathed nothing but dense smoke for days. Each time he saw her, his heart quickened—her soft green eyes; long, silky dark hair; olive complexion; and the scent of her.

It didn't matter that she had no money, no fancy clothes. He'd discovered not all women were like Martha Appleburg. What a relief that was to him! But, it was too late. He'd waited too long to open his eyes. And he'd made a promise to his father.

Sighing, he tore his gaze away from the sight before him, a soft, gentle woman in faded blue gingham. He could not have her. His lot in life was set, and it would be a miserable existence by all accounts.

If God is truly a God of mercy and compassion, he wondered, *how can this be happening?* James knew he hadn't been the best person he could have been, but he hadn't been the worst, either. Suddenly he lost any desire to pray again. What good would it do? His prayers seemed only to be ignored.

"Are you ready to go?" he asked.

Katelyn drew a deep breath, lifted her hair off her shoulders with both hands, and said, "As ready as I'll ever be."

James watched as she rounded Carrie and Toby up, hoisted them into the waiting wagon, and allowed him to lift her onto the buckboard step. She climbed into the back end atop pliable boards running lengthwise from the front to the rear axle. One of the mounted seats had been removed to haul the cots. Only when Katelyn and the two children were seated in the back did Martha step forward.

James lifted her up and in. She took her seat in front, her back stiff. He climbed aboard and slapped the reins against the necks of the two Cleveland bays pulling the wagon.

"Yaaa!" he yelled. They were off.

❧

The ride was bumpy and the morning breeze cool but comfortable. Katelyn glanced at Toby. He stayed quiet, peering around, seeming to know they were going home.

Katelyn had thought about this ahead of time. At first, she almost left Toby with her mother. Then it occurred to her that he might need to see his past home under different circumstances. She surmised it might soften the old memory, leave a less daunting image in his young mind. She would watch him closely for signs of distress.

Before long, they spotted the soddie on the horizon. Katelyn lifted her hand to cover her eyes from the sun and viewed the place. A smile lengthened her lips. She saw wagon after wagon and people milling about.

"They've come to help," James said in answer to her silent question.

"Have they all been vaccinated?"

"Most of them," James answered. "Some survived the smallpox some time ago, as children, and have a built-in immunity now."

"Thank You, Lord," Katelyn said out loud.

Her desire was to give life back to Cimarron. If she could save one life, she would succeed. Her goal was to save many, but she had to leave that in God's hands. She offered a silent prayer as they approached the homestead: *Father in heaven, I ask that You be with us as we seek to do Your will. Give us courage and strength that we may endure the agonies that lie ahead. And Father, please take care of little Toby. He needs You. In Jesus' name. Amen.*

"Whoa!" James tugged hard on the reins. The horses came to a halt, breathing heavily. He jumped down in one leap and stepped to the back of the wagon. Carrie greeted him with open arms, and he lifted her to the ground, then Toby, who didn't seem so eager to leave the safety of the buckboard.

James moved around front and lifted Martha safely to the ground, then Katelyn. Martha seemed fidgety.

"Are you all right?" James asked her.

Martha turned on him, and Katelyn couldn't believe the venom in the other woman's voice. "What are we doing here?"

James tried to explain the situation, but she wouldn't listen.

"You're crazy!" She turned to look at Katelyn. "You're both absolutely crazy!"

Clearing his throat and rubbing tired eyes, James said, "You don't have to go in, Martha. You can stay out here if you want."

"Of course I'll stay out here, you ninny!" She crossed her arms and stamped her foot. "Don't you realize that if we're exposed, we'll get the disease?" Martha glanced toward the soddie. "That place is full of smallpox!"

Removing his hat, James raked strong fingers through his tangle of black hair. "We've already been exposed, Martha, don't you understand? I've tried to explain that to you time and time again. We've already been exposed," he said slowly, emphasizing each word.

Katelyn stepped forward. Martha stepped back.

"Listen," Katelyn explained, trying to ignore the stab of pain Martha's act lodged inside her, "it's too late to worry about being exposed. Members of your family, mine, and James's have all suffered from the smallpox. We didn't know they had it, and we were unwittingly exposed as well." She hesitated, looking at James for reassurance. At his nod, she continued.

"The incubation period is about twelve days, Martha. This whole mess has only just begun. We can't do anything about ourselves, and we won't know whether we'll get it until that time is up. But we can do something to better the situation."

Martha tipped her nose at Katelyn. "I don't intend on getting it," she said. "When you two are writhing in agony with horrible little spots all over your faces, then I'll tell you that you should have heeded my warning."

Katelyn studied the ground, then the soddie. It was time to get moving. She couldn't get through to this woman. In a way, she felt sorry for her. Smallpox did not discriminate. It affected men and women, rich and poor. Hopefully Martha wouldn't come down with the disease. It might break her already weakened state of mind, if it didn't kill her.

"Come on, Toby," Katelyn called out. The boy placed his small hand inside hers. They walked into the house.

Carrie skipped to James's side and grasped two of his fingers, encircling them with her small hand. "Mon, James," she issued, giggling childishly.

How innocent the children are, he thought, tension melting away. He was glad Carrie had pulled through. Now, watching Katelyn, James was secretly thankful for the time he would have with her.

Shame suddenly filled him. He remembered. Martha would be his wife soon. He'd already spoken to her father, asked his blessing in taking her hand in marriage. No, he hadn't yet proposed to Martha, but he would. Soon. He had no doubt of what her answer would be. He wished he could have proposed to her first, but, with Gabe being sick, he had to do things a little differently.

His insides felt twisted in knots. What would a lifetime be like with Martha Appleburg? Her whining and complaining, her insolence, the way she made people feel when they were around her. Martha was not for him. Fate would see him forever destined to spend life with one woman while loving another. How could this have happened? Hot anger replaced the shame. He marched in after Katelyn.

Watching her calmed him somehow. Her charm and grace, her compassion and caring nature. She had so much inner beauty that lit up her face and filled her green eyes. She could wear a burlap sack, and it wouldn't detract from that inner radiance. James nearly laughed as this image flashed across his mind.

༈

Katelyn forced all her attention on the little boy holding her hand in an ever-tightening clench. "We're going to clean your house today, Toby. Okay?"

He nodded. "Where are my toys?"

Katelyn found it curious he didn't ask for members of his family. He knew. She didn't press the issue. Instead she looked back at James, a question on her face.

"Under the table," James answered. "I put all of them under the table."

Katelyn smiled as Toby released her hand and dashed to claim his toys.

Maggie Tolstoy approached Katelyn. "What do ya need done?" she asked. "Me and my two daughters come to hep out."

"Thank you so much, Maggie." Katelyn felt her eyes fill. She struggled to keep the tears from spilling freely down her cheeks. "You can start by washing everything down in the place. With soap and water. Even the walls," she added.

"We'll git right on it."

Katelyn watched as Maggie approached her daughters and told them something she couldn't hear. The three went to work. Others approached Katelyn, and she directed each to a task. A fire was needed in the hearth. Others took the bedding and washed it for use with the sick. Still others set about making candles from tallow or beeswax or whatever else might be available.

James had already directed some of the men to gather fuel for the fireplace. She noticed that he was busy building sockets along the walls to hold oil lamps and candles. Others continued making makeshift cots, while two men loaded a feather tick into a buckboard so they could transport patients like an ambulance might. The place buzzed with activity. Life.

Katelyn set about to boil the teas once an adequate fire blazed. Her attention was drawn to a corner of the room. Army blankets; quilts; and cotton, flannel, and muslin sheets sewn recently sat in several thick piles. Next to them, obviously brought in from the people swarming the property, rested tin plates, cups, pottery bowls, and sections of toweling stripped into small lengths for easier handling.

God had heard, Katelyn realized, and was providing all they might need. She mouthed a whispered "Thank You" and busied herself making beds. There were six cots lining the walls. More, once they were ready, would be placed side by side to allow plenty of room for the sick to rest. Katelyn knew more would be needed, but she didn't know where to put them. She could think about that problem later.

Just then Katelyn noticed Beth Jameston, the town seamstress, enter the dwelling. It was Beth, Katelyn believed, who was responsible for providing most of the blankets and sheets. Beth, her gray hair pulled back in a widow's bun and wearing a black dress, held several pies in her hands.

Approaching her, Katelyn relieved her of some of the load. "How are you, Beth?"

"Well as can be expected," said Beth, her mouth in that perpetually pinched form, as though somebody had squeezed it between their fingers and it had never regained its natural shape.

She shifted her load. "I've made meat pies, fruit pies, and biscuits. Got bread bakin' at home, some Brown Betty, and a big pot of rabbit stew cookin'. Wanted to get these fixin's to you soon as possible."

Bottom lip trembling, Katelyn embraced her in a generous hug. "Thank you so much, Beth. You're an angel!"

"Least I can do." Beth wiped a hand across her forehead, clearing beads of sweat away. "I'll supply the food and blankets, even gowns if need be," she offered. "Got other women cookin' too. And sewin'. Would you be needin' anythin' else?"

"Not at the moment."

"Let me know if you do; we'll work it out." She hesitated. "Wanted to tell you, we know what yer doin' for this town, and we're much obliged."

Katelyn wanted to tell her she hadn't done anything yet

but didn't. She just smiled through her tears and watched Beth set her pies on the table before taking her leave.

James stepped in, a patch of sweat having formed along his neckline and down his chest, darkening his gray flannel shirt. Sleeves rolled up, hair wild, jeans filthy, he was still an attractive vision to Katelyn. She forced her mind to focus on the details that needed her attention.

"We're ready to get the first load," he announced. "There are some families who have nobody to care for them."

"Start there," said Katelyn. "Bring those who are sick and alone." She thought for a moment. "You may have to go house to house, business to business."

"Intend to," replied James. "We'll be back soon." He turned to go but swung around to face Katelyn again, as though forgetting something.

"What is it?" she asked.

"I'll bring additional supplies from the mercantile. Anything in particular you might be needing?"

"Not sure just yet. Seems I have most everything." Then she remembered. "Do the Fontanna's have a milk cow?"

"Yes, saw her out by the stable."

"We'll be needing milk."

"I'll have one of the boys get right on it." He stepped to the door, ready to make his exit.

Suddenly, Katelyn's eyes widened. "That's it!"

"What's it?"

"We're gonna be okay!" she exclaimed jubilantly. "We're gonna be okay!"

"What do you mean?"

"James," Katelyn rushed, "have you milked cows before?"

"Of course."

"Do you think Toby has?"

"I'd bet my last shiner on it. Most boys his age have."

"Do you know what cowpox is?"

"Yeah, I know. Got it once. Cows had it, and I got this strange rash on my hands."

"Me, too! I had it, too!"

"What does that have to do with anything?"

"James, it's the reason we won't get smallpox. Don't you understand?"

He moved back inside, closer to Katelyn. "No, maybe you'd better explain."

seven

"Call Toby in first," Katelyn whispered excitedly. "I need to question him."

James brought the little boy to face Katelyn.

She dropped to one knee in front of the child so she could view him eye to eye. "Toby, have you milked cows before?"

His nod sent a surge of excitement running through her body like floodwaters. "Did you ever get something on your hands, like bumps, from milking the cows?"

Again, Toby nodded affirmatively. "My papa called it the cowpox," he recalled.

Katelyn stood and tussled his hair with one hand. "Good boy. You can go back outside and play now."

"Can I have a biscuit?" He shot his brown gaze to the table laden with food, expectation showing on his dirt-streaked face.

Stepping to the table, Katelyn retrieved two biscuits, still warm, from a basket covered by a blue-checked cloth. "Give one to Carrie, okay?"

Toby grabbed the food from her hands, smiled, and darted from the house.

Glancing at James, Katelyn noted the puzzled expression on his face hadn't changed.

"Milker's nodules," she said matter-of-factly. "I don't know why I didn't realize this before. Would have saved a lot of worry."

"I still don't understand."

"Let me explain," Katelyn offered. "Cowpox is a pox virus, and doctors discovered that people who developed cowpox also developed an immunity to smallpox. It's the strain used in the vaccine."

"So. . .because I've had 'milker's nodules' I won't have to

worry about getting the smallpox?"

"That's right."

"Are you sure?"

"Yes."

Katelyn could easily see the relief that filled James at the news. Then a look of worry crossed his face. "Do you think Martha's ever milked a cow?" he asked.

Crossing her arms over her chest as though chilled, Katelyn said, "I don't know, James."

She was touched by his concern. Although she hoped Martha had experienced the cowpox, she thought it unlikely. The wealthy had servants for that sort of thing. All Martha had to worry about was eating, sleeping, and looking beautiful. It also occurred to Katelyn for the first time that such a life could be miserable.

Katelyn couldn't imagine a day without doing *something*. From sunrise to sunset, when she accomplished much, a certain contentment filled her. It was by her own hands that many drew comfort. And she, in turn, drew comfort from the efforts of others around her.

Just as now. The community donated food and blankets; people cleaned and built what was needed. All the necessities had been provided to make this tiny sod home into a miniature hospital. Katelyn knew she could not have achieved all this by herself.

Did Martha ever get a sense of peace such as this after hard and steady work? Katelyn viewed her labors as giving her wealth—not in a monetary sense, but in a spiritual sense. It was true. Of course, having money would be nice and make some things easier; but Katelyn knew, money or not, she would still use her hands, develop her talents, and serve others.

She remembered the words of Romans 14:17-19: "For the kingdom of God is not food and drink, but righteousness and peace and joy in the Holy Spirit. For he who serves Christ in these things is acceptable to God and approved by men. Therefore let us pursue the things which make for peace and the things by which one may edify another."

James interrupted her thoughts. "Better go talk with Martha for a moment."

"Go right ahead, James. I'll get things ready for the first group."

He left, leaving Katelyn to wonder at her newfound understanding. Still, something nagged at her conscience. *Do I really have the skill to doctor the sick? Or am I just fooling myself?* She gave herself a mental shake. *Faith. Have faith.*

But no matter how she tried, Katelyn couldn't get her questions about her abilities to leave. They continually dug into her conscience like the dull blade of a knife. She could only continue making beds, boiling teas, and cleaning. Time would soon enough reveal how skilled she was.

She moved to the smudged window and peeked out, watching as James walked away from Martha, his head hanging low. She knew the answer to his question. Martha was not immune. All Katelyn could do was pray, hoping the young woman might be spared, wanting everybody to be spared, if possible. Then she resumed her duties, trying not to think beyond the present.

≥∞

Many of the workers went home late in the morning to tend their sick loved ones. Nearly every person who showed up to help had either lost a family member or had to care for somebody with the smallpox. Some promised to return daily to offer assistance.

Katelyn wondered if a quarantine within the town would help, given that so many people had been exposed. More likely, the entire town needed to be under quarantine to protect travelers and the other towns where they might spread the deadly disease. Katelyn determined to speak with James about the issue as soon as the opportunity arose.

The sound of horses' hooves beating the hard prairie ground and the squeak of wagon wheels told Katelyn the first of the sick had arrived. She wiped her hands on the apron fastened around her waist. It was about to begin. Katelyn took a deep breath, tucked stray tresses of dark, glossy hair behind her ears, and opened the door.

The wagon had come to a stop in front of the temporary hospital. Men lifted the sick, one by one, and carried them inside. Each patient was placed gently on the crudely built cots. Katelyn walked behind, removing boots and shoes and covering the fevered, shivering forms with blankets.

The agony of these sick people was intense, and Katelyn's heart went out to them. Two children cried. A man and woman moaned. Eventually she might get used to the sight, but now it was almost more than she could bear. "Lord, help me," she whispered.

She felt the gentle press on her shoulder. Katelyn spun around to see James's eyes filled with tears.

"Are you doing all right, Kate?"

"Are you?" she responded.

"Just reminds me of my father," he whispered.

She touched his shoulder briefly. "Let it out, James; it's okay."

Although James fought, the tears came, like a flood. Instinctively, Katelyn pulled his head down to her shoulder. She rubbed his hair gently, marveling at its softness. "That's good. Very good, James."

Her own tears spilled down her cheeks, drops of agony, as she remembered her loved ones and as she ached for James and his pain. It was good he mourned now, she thought. Otherwise, his grief would find a different way out that might not be so easy to handle.

Within minutes, the onslaught of grief ended. Moans from the sick filled the air, causing Katelyn and James to realize they had to press on. James placed his hat back on his head and left without a word to get more people.

In a sense, Katelyn felt honored that he had allowed her to see his pain in a way other people might never witness. He trusted her. The thought warmed her, like a tiny flame providing warmth to her spirit.

Dabbing her cheeks with the back of one hand, Katelyn sniffed. Then she gripped the water bucket, which held fresh water from the well, grabbed several sections of toweling from the pile in the corner, and set to work.

Sitting on the edge of each cot, she dipped a segment of cloth in the cool liquid, wrung it out, and secured one piece on every forehead.

Next she filled tin cups with the fever-fighting tea and made every effort to drain at least some of it into the mouths of the ill. She pulled the blankets back up around their shoulders and stoked the fire continuously to fight their constant chills.

Katelyn also said a prayer at each bedside, a prayer for healing and for her own strength to endure. Then she continued her preparations for the next group of patients, hoping they would have enough cots for everyone.

That completed, Katelyn stepped outside to check on Carrie and Toby. They played contentedly by poking sticks in the prairie dog holes, trying to chase one of the tiny creatures out. Though unsuccessful, they laughed gleefully and jumped up and down in their childlike exuberance. It pleased Katelyn that they got along so well. Carrie needed a friend. So did Toby.

She surveyed the area around the buildings to see what had become of Martha. The woman was nowhere in sight. Scanning the area once more, Katelyn noticed one of the Fontanna mules was missing. The other grazed nearby, close to the milk cow.

Did she go home to her family? Katelyn wondered. The Appleburgs certainly needed her. With one servant ill as well as Martha's baby sister, father, and mother, the family would need help. Otherwise, the Appleburgs would have to be brought to the temporary hospital. Martha wouldn't like that, Katelyn was sure.

Curiosity gripped her. How long had Martha been gone? Her concern increased when she saw dust on the horizon. The wagon. But where was Martha?

ames spent the next hour unloading the people and settling
hem in their beds. As soon as the wagon was empty and the
orses taken care of, James collapsed at the kitchen table, his
ead in his arms. He was totally exhausted, but he feared
what would happen if he allowed himself any rest. Too much
was happening. Too many deaths to absorb. Too much
ragedy.

He heard a noise and looked up. Katelyn had stepped to
he bench and sat down beside him. A quick glance told him
hat most of the patients were sleeping, although one still
moaned. The children clawed at their sores in their sleep.

Katelyn's green eyes were filled with concern as she looked
t him. "You're only human, James. You have to rest now."

"Can't. Too much to do."

"We can start again later this evening. But right now, you
need something to eat, and you need some rest."

"Too much to do," he repeated.

"I'll fix us each a plate, and one for Toby and Carrie. Then
you *must* get some sleep."

James watched as Katelyn got up, gathered four tin plates,
and loaded them with meat pie, fruit pie, and a biscuit each.

"What about you?" James asked, watching her work.

Katelyn managed a smile. "I slept last night; you didn't."

James took the plate without argument and ate.

Katelyn called Toby and Carrie inside, gave them each
their food, and sent them out onto the front porch.

She sat down, ate a bite of pork pie, and swallowed it
down with fresh milk. "Where's Martha?" she asked. As if in
answer to her question, they heard a commotion outside. A
buggy pulled up.

Martha's laughter rang clear as a school bell. Both James
and Katelyn left their plates and hurried outdoors.

James was appalled by what he saw. Martha scrambled
down off the wagon and struggled to dislodge her black skirt
from between one wheel and the buggy frame. The more

difficulty she had, the more uncontrollably she laughed.

James stepped to her, offering assistance. He wasn't quite sure what was causing her insane laughter until he moved closer. The scent on her breath. Alcohol. Martha had been drinking.

"Let me help you," he said, easily freeing the material from its tangle in the wheel.

Martha stumbled and nearly fell. James caught her beneath her arm and held her steady. A sigh of exasperation left his lips. "Martha, what did you have?"

"Oh, Jamesh, nothing really," Martha replied, the alcohol adding a slur to her southern drawl. "Just a bit of champagne ish all." She laughed, as though the thought struck her funny.

"We need to get you home, girl, so you can rest." James peered into eyes that harbored a familiar drowsy look. He wondered why she had done this to herself; thought maybe the stress of everything, the torment, got to be too much.

Just then, Katelyn walked up to where the two stood. James watched as she looped an arm around Martha's shoulders. "Are you hungry, Martha?" she asked.

Good, James thought, *food will help Martha sober up.* To his astonishment, Martha allowed Katelyn to lead her to the porch and help her sit down. He was struck by Katelyn's ability to take control of the situation, even with all that was going on around them.

Oh, Lord, I love this woman. The revelation didn't surprise him. But he could only love her from afar, probably for the rest of his life. How complicated this situation had become. How could he possibly endure the life of misery and loneliness that lay ahead? Surely God was merciful.

In desperation, he offered up a silent prayer: *Dear Father, I'm not sure what good this will do, but I'm going to try again. I'm asking something for myself. I know I made a promise, and I intend to keep that promise. But if there's any way out, I'm asking for that. If there's any way out at all, please allow it to be. In Jesus' name, Amen."*

He set his sights on Katelyn again. She slipped inside, retrieved her tin of food, made her way out, and handed the plate to Martha.

"Try and eat," she urged. "It'll make you feel better."

Martha managed to fit chunks of pork pie into her mouth, chewing slowly, swallowing hard. When Martha had eaten her fill, Katelyn dropped to one knee beside the woman.

"Martha," she started, "what caused you to do this?"

Suddenly, Martha began to cry. Katelyn leaned forward and wrapped her in a gentle hug, rocking her slowly, like a baby. Soon the cries turned to wrenching sobs.

All James could do was watch. He listened to Katelyn's next words.

"Martha," she began after the sobs subsided, "you just have to trust God."

"I'm trying to," Martha offered between sniffles.

Her words were less garbled. James assumed the food had accomplished this. He felt sorry for Martha—knew exactly what she felt. But she shouldn't have drowned her troubles in drink.

Katelyn spoke again. "Trust in the Lord with all your heart, and lean not on your own understanding; In all your ways acknowledge Him, and He shall direct your paths."

James's eyes widened. Those words! They were meant for him as well. He knew it as surely as if a silent voice had told him so. And hadn't they come just after he'd offered up his silent prayer?

Maybe God *was* listening, after all. Still, James couldn't allow himself to get his hopes up. But he would do what the verses suggested: *Trust in the Lord.*

You direct my paths, Lord, James prayed. *I'm leaving everything in Your hands. This is a load I simply cannot carry alone.*

Katelyn stood, her eyes reflecting concern.

"What is it?" James asked.

For a moment, Katelyn just looked at him, as though she

had no voice. Finally she spoke.

"James," she nearly choked, "Martha's got the fever. You must take her home where somebody can begin caring for her."

eight

James reined in the horses to an easy stop. Martha had slept the entire distance, leaning up against his shoulder. He had never felt this tired, this drained before, but every time he thought he might get some shut-eye, some new dilemma arose. This time the problem was Martha.

He peered back, checking on his paint tethered to the rear of the wagon. James knew he'd need a ride back to the Fontanna homestead once he returned Martha home with her buggy.

Gently, James lifted the sleeping woman onto his lap. With her in his arms, he managed to step down from the carriage. After securing the horses, he made his way up the porch steps to the frosted glass door. It stood slightly ajar, an alarmingly unusual occurrence at the Appleburg home.

With his left boot, James nudged the door open wider and stepped inside with his burden. The Victorian furnishings, normally polished to a sheen, were lightly covered with dust. Pillows from the settee had been tossed askew, and one lay in the middle of the floor.

A vase of feathers rested on the edge of a mahogany table instead of in the center. *Harper's Weekly, Scribner's Monthly,* and *The Saturday Evening Post* sat awry on the white marble top.

His concern mounted. Things didn't feel right.

"Hello!" he called out. "Anybody home?"

Martha grew heavy in his arms. After a minute had elapsed and nobody answered, James set Martha down on the gold tapestry upholstered settee. She slept like an exhausted child. Fever made her cheeks rosy. After inserting a pillow beneath her head, he strode through the maze of rooms, trying to find somebody. Anybody.

"Hello!" he called out again and again, each time feeling a greater sense of urgency. Finally, just beyond the parlor, he heard a voice.

"Come in, come in," said a woman, whose voice James did not recognize.

"Where?" James asked. "Where are you?"

"In the kitchen."

The aroma of cooked meat led James to the kitchen door. A rush of heat greeted him when he opened the door. An older woman busied herself at the stove. On her head rested a tiny white hat. Her hair had been pulled back into a widow's bun, so tight it made her features appear stretched. She wore a blue dress enveloped in a white ruffled apron.

"Everyone's taken ill," she said, not looking up at her visitor, nor seeming to care that a stranger entered her space.

"Everyone?"

"Yes, everyone." Wiping her hands on the apron, she bent and tugged the oven door open. With a towel, she retrieved two loaves of bread, their tops baked to a golden brown. She let the door swing shut.

"I'm preparing the evening meal," she told James.

Something wasn't right with the woman, James thought. If everybody was sick with the smallpox, why was she preparing the evening meal? For whom?

"You're welcome to join us," she invited, icing a saddle of mutton with a topping of cooled meat drippings. Next, she crowned the meat with a coronet of peeled vegetable flowers and a sprig of curled parsley.

"Are you alone?" he asked.

"Surely am," she stated. "Surely am."

"Where are the others? Who's caring for them?"

The woman stirred the contents of a kettle on top of the stove. James studied his surroundings. Dried herbs and spices hung from the arched rafters in the kitchen. Positioned against the back wall was a long oak table holding a ball of dough with a spilling of white flour beneath it. A Windsor chair, with its plank seat, spindled back, and canted legs, sat against the wall opposite the table.

He spotted a barrel of pork by the wall nearest the washroom. Tins of coffee, vegetables, and sacks of flour and cornmeal covered shelves above and around the stove, within easy reach. He recognized these as having been purchased from his own store. Some items he didn't recognize, though. James regained his focus and realized the woman hadn't answered his question.

"Who's caring for the others?" he repeated.

"Doin' best I can," she mumbled.

Clearing his throat and growing increasingly tense, James said, "I'm sure you're doing a good job." He paused. "All this cooking and caring for the sick is hard work."

Suddenly his admiration for Katelyn grew despite himself. Images of her seemed to hover at the edges of his memory. Rubbing at his left temple in an effort to clear his thoughts, he wondered what to do next.

"Who will eat this food?" he asked, surprising even himself with the question. Forward and to-the-point had always been part of his nature, but never as far as women were concerned. They were the gentle sex and must be treated gently, James believed.

The startled look in the woman's face told James he had finally gotten through to her. He watched as she dabbed tears from her eyes.

"Listen," he offered, approaching her, "why don't you bring all this fare and come with me?"

"Where?" She dabbed at her eyes again.

"To the Fontanna homestead."

"Ain't all them folks passed on?"

"All except one," James issued. "We're using the place as a hospital. Katelyn McKnight is leading the efforts. She needs help from people like you, people who can cook and clean and help her tend the sick."

James thought he detected a measure of relief covering her taut features.

"Can we take Mr. and Mrs. Appleburg? And little Maggie? And—"

"We'll take them all," James interrupted. "We'll take them all." He thought for a second. "Can you drive a buckboard?"

"Certainly can, with the best of 'em."

"Good." He rubbed his left temple again. "You gather the food so it won't be wasted. We'll have workers tomorrow who can use the nourishment. I'm going to hitch the horses to the wagon. We'll be needing feather ticking to make the Appleburgs and the servants as comfortable as possible during the ride."

Within forty minutes, all was in order. James carried each person out, one by one, in his arms. He retrieved Martha last and positioned her as before, leaning against him for support. One of the sick rested in the rear of the buggy on a pallet of blankets. The buckboard carried the others.

James made a mental note to contact his good friend and confidant John Dorman, owner of Cimarron's livery stable, to see if he might help out with the Appleburg livestock. Longhorn cattle grazed near the creek. The horses would need extra attention. And the family dog, a yellow Labrador, must be cared for.

His exhaustion turned to restlessness. James wondered if he would sleep at all.

੪

After applying the crushed leaves of the yellow dock to as many smallpox lesions as possible, Katelyn offered drinks to everyone. Some fought, but she managed to get a little water into each person.

They created beds on the floor for the Appleburg group until more cots could be built. The supply of blankets dwindled. That would have to be dealt with. Food, so far, was plentiful.

Lastly, Katelyn stepped to where Martha lay, crying softly. She bent over her.

"Martha," she whispered, "it's going to be all right."

Gently, she smoothed tendrils of the woman's beautiful blond ringlets back and away from her face. Katelyn removed the black riding habit Martha wore and pulled on a more comfortable flannel sleeping shirt. Then she snugged the blankets up around the sick woman's shoulders.

When Martha didn't respond, Katelyn stood. She rubbed the small of her back, which had started aching. Then she stepped to the window and looked out. To her utter relief, James finally slept outside on the porch, his Stetson pulled over his eyes. His feet were crossed at the ankles, hands folded together over a flat stomach.

Peering into the western sky, she grew mesmerized by the sunset bathing the horizon in a cascade of orange and lavender radiance. The huge ball of fire that warmed their days edged its way down, ever so slowly. Katelyn was certain she could see it move, if she watched it steady enough.

A child's cries reached her ears, followed by several pleading moans. Katelyn turned back to her work. The process began again: cool, wet cloths for their foreheads; sassafras tea for fevers; and powdered yellow dock or wild pansy leaves applied to sores.

Katelyn wondered when she might rest. She also worried about her mother being left alone for such a long time. Katelyn knew her mother was a strong woman, a smart woman, but still she wondered. Maybe tomorrow somebody would spell her and she could go home for a little while, see her mother, maybe get some much-needed rest.

Darkness fell within the half-hour. Katelyn rounded up Toby and Carrie, who were busy playing games of hide-and-seek. The two children were not eager to go to bed, so Katelyn had to insist that they sleep. It had been a long, hard day for everyone. She had made two extra pallets for the little ones. Now, she tucked them in and sang lullabies to take their minds off the pitiful cries echoing around them.

Once the children fell sound asleep, quiet suddenly filled the makeshift hospital. Nobody moaned or cried. Her heart thumped hard in her chest. Quickly she shuffled to each person, checking for life. All was fine.

Katelyn didn't know what to make of it. A memory hit her like a well-aimed bullet. She remembered singing to little Carrie and how the girl quieted more with each melody. She'd test the theory later. Right now, hunger pangs sent her to the kitchen.

She sliced off a section of mutton brought from the Appleburg home. Such a dish! Katelyn had never eaten something so rich before. Adding a biscuit, she savored the delicious meal. The food brought on a sleepy edge she couldn't shake.

While everyone else rested, Katelyn leveled herself onto the hard pine bench beside the table. There weren't any blankets left to create a pallet, so she used her arm as a pillow. Within minutes she fell into blissful sleep.

Katelyn woke with a start. She stood and made her way to the sound that had roused her. A child cried out for his mother. Positioning herself on the edge of the cot, Katelyn lifted the four-year-old boy into her arms and rocked him, as a mother might. The child soon drifted back to sleep.

Every time Katelyn sought to return him to his bed, he cried out. In response, she pulled him to her, wishing the sun would return. She hadn't been able to sleep very long. Didn't matter, she surmised. Tomorrow might bring the promise of rest when the others returned.

The sound of a voice gave her such a jolt, she jumped and the boy was startled awake.

"Sorry," said James, coming around to stand in front of her beside the cot.

Before long, as Katelyn rocked, the child slipped back to sleep.

"That's okay." Peering up at him, she struggled to see his eyes. Candles provided little light. James's presence provided a secure, warm feeling Katelyn couldn't begin to measure or understand.

Stop it, she warned herself. *He belongs to another.* The

thought left an ache in her heart. She glanced in Martha's direction, then back to James, finally resting her gaze on the little boy she held in her arms.

"I'm glad you were able to get some rest," she told James, breaking the silence hovering between them.

Rubbing the back of his neck, he said, "It helped. What little I got."

"Feel better now?"

"Much."

"Good, that's very good, James."

Rubbing his neck again, James asked, "Want to step out on the porch, get some fresh air?"

Katelyn thought for a moment. "That would be nice." With James's aid, she settled the child back in his blankets. He whimpered. Katelyn hummed softly. Then he drifted off to sleep.

James reached out to grip her elbow, but Katelyn pulled back. That wouldn't be right, she believed. Besides, it would only add to her struggles over the man.

Without a word, James turned and led the way out to the porch. He peered up at the stars as though studying the constellations.

Katelyn didn't wish to hurt his feelings but believed she must guard herself. She knew, without doubt, she was falling in love. For the first time! And she felt ripped in two at the situation she faced.

It was Martha who would marry James. Martha who would bear his children. Martha who would know his love and gentleness. All of it seemed so terribly wrong!

She knew Martha could never love this man as she, herself, could. A heaviness settled inside her.

Martha and James would be very sad should they marry. There was no evidence of attraction between them. They never gazed at each other with captivating glances, never displayed anything resembling a blossoming love.

After a moment's silence, James spoke. "I wanted to

apologize for what happened earlier."

She knew of what he spoke. "There's no cause for that, James. You needed to cry. We all do, James. We're human."

A slight grin crossed his lips.

You're so right for me! she wanted to scream, miserable at the injustice of it all. Again, she chastised herself. Then, the Scripture she'd recited earlier to Martha returned: *Trust in the Lord with all your heart, and lean not on your own understanding.*

All right, Father, You're in charge, she prayed. She turned her attention back to James, struggling vainly to deny her emotions.

"I've cried, too, James, when nobody was around to dry my tears." She thought she saw the meager smile fade and hoped she hadn't upset him.

"I wish I could have been there with you to dry your tears, Katelyn, just as you did mine."

This is impossible, Lord! Did you hear what he just said? She wondered how she could possibly avoid falling deeply in love with him, only to watch him wed another. James was the most compassionate man she'd ever met. He was intelligent, inspiring, his spirit indomitable. The man embraced his duties and faced challenges head on. His very presence provided her with strength she might not have been able to claim on her own.

Katelyn knew the Lord worked through people, but why was He working through James to help her? Didn't He know what was taking place in her heart? How could He allow this to continue if He knew her heart?

Circumstances beyond their control brought them together. Maybe circumstances would separate them. She wanted to hope for that, but couldn't. Katelyn needed to be near James. The thought caused her conscience to battle with itself like swordsmen fighting to the death.

"Did you hear me, Katelyn?"

Her cheeks flushed red with embarrassment. *I'm glad it's*

dark. In her thoughts she'd forgotten all about him.

"Yes, I did. B–but I got through it. The Lord spared my mother and baby sister. I'm not alone, and I'm thankful for that." How she wished he'd been able to dry her tears. Only him. Only James Connor, the dark stranger that entered her confused little life, causing even more confusion than ever.

James continued. "Katy, I sense you don't trust yourself."

Her breath caught in her throat. "W–what do you mean?" Surely he hadn't noticed her struggle over her feelings toward him. Was it that noticeable?

"I mean, I think you doubt yourself on caring for these people."

Katelyn sighed with relief. "Well, I don't have the skill my mother has," she explained.

"Maybe not, Katy, but you have your own skills, and they're developing. I think you're doing a fine job."

She loved it when he called her Katy. Few people did. It created a more personal friendship, if one could call it that. Yes, friendship. That's all this was, a developing friendship. Something inside told Katelyn that wasn't so, though she fought to believe it was.

"What if I fail?" She heard the words leave her lips and wished she could retrieve them. Sharing her insecurities made her feel vulnerable.

James was quick to reply. "You won't fail, Katy. If you do your best, then you haven't failed. If you don't try, you will have failed."

His words made perfect sense, but she still felt uneasy about her new role. "I've never had to handle a situation like this. Mother should be the one in charge here. She's the more capable person."

"But, you were chosen for the task, not Abigail."

"Why would the Lord choose me and not my mother?"

Clearing his throat, James responded, "He has His reasons."

Katelyn sensed a certain tension in his words. Was he angry with God? Some people responded to trauma that way.

She changed the subject.

"I'm sorry Martha has taken ill," she said. She certainly didn't want to push God on James. His relationship with the Father had to be his own choice.

She watched as he dropped his eyes to the wood rail surrounding the porch. He tugged at his hat. "I'm sorry, too," he said.

"She'll be okay, James. You must believe that."

He didn't answer.

A lump formed in Katelyn's throat. Had she said too much? Too little? She took a deep breath and added, "You'll s–still be able to marry her, James."

"I haven't proposed marriage, yet," he answered.

A tiny measure of hope found its way into Katelyn's heart. He hadn't proposed. Not yet! Had he decided against it? Had she been right about them all along?

"I didn't know," was all she could think to say. The lump in her throat seemed to grow larger. She decided to address a more comfortable issue. "I've been meaning to speak with you about something, James."

He stood straighter, as though thankful for a new topic. "What's that, Katy?"

"The quarantine we discussed earlier is not going to work."

"I know."

His response surprised her. He'd obviously been thinking about the same thing.

She continued, peering at his profile as he studied the night sky. "Many in the town are infected. We need to quarantine all of Cimarron, send telegrams and couriers to surrounding communities to stay away for now. And we need to be sure our people don't stray, don't travel anywhere where they might infect others and start this whole mess someplace else."

"I hate the thought of cutting ourselves off, but we may have to," James agreed. "The reason most Cimarron folk didn't receive their vaccinations is because they were busy moving here and settling in. Folks in surrounding towns may be in the same situation."

"That's true, James, and I don't think we can afford to risk it. Many are venturing west, even now." Katelyn drew a deep breath.

"I agree," said James, turning to face Katelyn.

His towering form made Katelyn want to hide in his shadow, feeling as though safety and comfort resided there. "Can you direct the quarantine efforts?" she asked.

"I'll get on it first thing in the morning. You just concentrate on your end. Anything else needs doing, I'll do it. Okay?"

"Okay." That was easy enough.

Their conversation ended when Martha screamed out in her sleep. Katelyn turned to reenter the soddie, but James put a restraining hand on her shoulder.

"I'll go to her," he said. "She's frightened is all."

When he left, Katelyn rested both palms on the post in front of her and breathed deeply of the cool night air. So, James hadn't proposed, she mused. A giddy sensation overtook her. She had been right. James and Martha were not a match. They didn't fit with each other.

Another thought bothered her, though. James never said he didn't intend on proposing marriage, just that he hadn't yet. She wrapped her arms around herself, feeling suddenly chilled, and made her way inside.

☙

Sleep evaded Katelyn as she cared for one, then another, throughout the night. The sun rose, its amber light filtering into corners of the soddie. People woke, needing attention. About midmorning, workers arrived. Sounds of hammers pounding nails and axes hacking wood cheered her after listening to nothing but moans all night.

Beth returned wearing a fresh cinnamon-colored dress. She approached Katelyn, who was busy brewing tea and creating paste poultices.

"Good morning," Katelyn greeted her. "How are you?"

Smiling, Beth answered, "All mine's fine."

Katelyn's heart jumped in her chest. "I'm so happy for you, Beth, so very, very happy!" She easily remembered her own relief when her mother and Carrie had pulled through.

Surrounding her in a hug, Beth told her, "I'm here to spell ya, if'n ya be needin' to git home for a time. Surely that mother of your'n could use the sight of ya."

Without hesitation, Katelyn briefed Beth on what needed to be done: water boiled, blankets washed, feedings, medicines applied to sores, fevers brought down. She spoke so fast, Beth broke into giggles.

"I'll just do what I can 'til ya git back," she told Katelyn. "Ya can leave them younguns here if'n ya want."

"Thank you, so much, Beth!" She glanced around her, hoping to locate James, then remembered he rode into town to establish the quarantine measures.

She turned to face Beth again. "If James returns, please tell him where I've gone. And that I'll be back soon."

"Will do."

Making her way outside, Katelyn saddled a mule and headed home. She hadn't realized how much she missed her mother or her home until she saw it again. Excitement welled within her at the thought of seeing her mother again. She had so much to discuss with her and so many questions.

They hadn't lost anybody during the night. The dawn had brought a beautiful day. A few billowy clouds flirted in the blue sky overhead, and Katelyn's spirits soared.

nine

The homestead appeared as Katelyn had left it. A few clothes hung on the line, mostly her mother's dresses, some flannel nightshirts, and bedding. *Mama must be feeling better,* she thought.

Katelyn's eyes were drawn to the graves, but she quickly tore her gaze away. The time would come when she'd visit them. Not now.

Her mother met her at the door, a lovely smile lighting her serene features. She was dressed in bright blue gingham. Her hair had been pulled back in a loose bun with tendrils dangling about her face. Katelyn noted her cheeks had a healthy glow to them.

They embraced, each not wanting to turn loose of the other. After a few moments, her mother squeezed Katelyn about the shoulders and released her grip.

"Daughter, I've missed you." Tears formed in her green eyes, despite the smile.

Katelyn stepped back and studied her mother intently. "I've missed you, too. How are you feeling?"

"Doing much, much better. Feel like my strength is returning, although slower than I'd like. Can't seem to catch my breath."

"Takes time, Mama, but you mustn't overdo it." Katelyn knew how much her mother hated being still even for short periods of time. She always insisted on have something to do, something to occupy herself.

They both stepped into the soddie. The scent of sage reached Katelyn's nostrils. "Smells good."

"Thought I'd make this a pleasant home again."

"Good, that's very good."

Her mother chuckled.

"What?" Katelyn questioned, her brows slanting in toward her nose.

"You always say that: 'Good, that's very good.' "

Katelyn's smile faded. "I'm sorry. I didn't know I did that, said that, all the time."

"No, no, no, sweetheart. It's what I love about you. It's part of who you are." She paused. "Don't ever change it. Promise?"

"I promise." The smile returned. Katelyn glanced around the place. The dishes had been washed, and fresh water boiled in the pot over the hearth. The bed was made. Newly picked herbs and various other plants dried on the windowsill.

"How's Carrie?" Mama asked, changing the subject. "I miss my baby so."

Katelyn stepped to the table and sat down on the pine bench, weariness setting in. "She's doing real good, Mama. She and Toby play and laugh all day long. They get along so well. She's happy again, and she has *all* her energy back."

"Isn't it funny how children can just bounce back from the worst of experiences, while it takes us adults a longer time of it?" Katelyn's mother pushed a tendril back, tucking the strand of hair beneath her bun.

"It is strange," Katelyn agreed, "but that's how children are."

"I'm glad for that."

"Me, too," Katelyn agreed, secretly wishing adults could be as resilient.

Mama took a seat beside Katelyn and studied her eyes. "Now," she said, "tell me everything."

Katelyn recapped the events as she remembered them, leaving out her emotional struggles and doubts.

"It's been a hard ordeal for you, I know," her mother said, "but it sounds as though you're handling it very well." She hesitated. "I am so proud of you, Daughter. So proud."

But Katelyn didn't want her mother to be proud just yet. Her accomplishments, as far as she was concerned, had been minimal. She changed the subject.

"Mama, I need to talk with you about some things that are bothering me." Katelyn stared at a floorboard as her feelings rushed back. She knew she could talk to her mother about anything. They had a unique bond.

"What is it? I'm listening." Mama gripped Katelyn's hand and held it in her own, offering reassurance. Then she let it go and seemed to study her daughter.

Katelyn's words rushed out as if they had a life of their own. "First of all, I'm not sure I can do as good a job as you. I'm afraid I might fail, if you must know the truth."

Mama lifted a hand in the air, stopping the flow of words. "Honey, just do the best job you can. That's all the Lord expects of you." Her hand dropped to her lap, and she clasped her hands together. "If you do that, you won't fail."

Just as James said, Katelyn thought.

"I *will* do the best job I can. I just feel inadequate, somehow. I don't have the experience you have."

"It takes doing to gain experience, and after this is over and done, you will be well equipped to handle anything that comes your way." She gazed at Katelyn, touched her hand for a brief second. "In a way, this is good. It will prepare you. You have to learn fast, gain knowledge in a short amount of time. I wish I had the same experience when I was starting out."

"Really?"

"Yes, really. Remember, our Lord works everything to good for those who love Him. But what else is on your heart? Something else is bothering you, and I don't think it has anything to do with the smallpox."

Astonishment filled Katelyn's eyes. How did her mother know?

Katelyn grew silent, trying to find the right words to say what she must.

"Mama, I think. . .uh uh, I know I'm in love."

Her mother's eyes lit up. "That's wonderful!"

"You don't know the half of it. This is not as simple as it seems."

She saw concern edging the glow away in her mother's eyes.

"Go ahead," her mother urged.

"Well. . .it seems he's involved with somebody else, except I'm not so sure now. Sometimes I am, other times I'm not." She glanced at the ceiling, which was meshed with cheesecloth to keep the rains out.

"I'm listening," her mother coaxed.

Katelyn rested her gaze on her mother. "It's James Connor, Mama. He's the man I've fallen in love with."

"Doesn't surprise me," her mother responded. "I remember parts of when he was here, heard his voice several times when I woke. Watched him while I sat in the rocker. He's attracted to you, Katelyn. I can see it."

"It's. . .it's just that I don't know whether he intends to wed Martha Appleburg or not. It seems the two don't get along, don't seem to fit together."

"Did you ask him?"

"In a manner of speaking, but not directly."

"Well?"

"He neither denied it, nor admitted to it."

"There's your answer."

Confused, Katelyn drew in her bottom lip. "Mama, they've been courting for nearly a year now. That says it all. Doesn't it?"

"Not necessarily." Mama smiled. "You have to hear the truth of things, not what you *think* you hear."

"But I am," said Katelyn. "I–I mean I think I am."

"Try to listen with your heart, Katelyn, and the truth will be revealed. Don't jump to conclusions."

"But, what if it isn't so? What if he *is* planning to wed Martha but hasn't proposed yet due to the epidemic and Martha being sick and all."

"That might be possible, but it's doubtful. The way you said he responded doesn't sound like he's in love with the Appleburg girl."

"It doesn't seem like love to me. Still, nothing has been confirmed either way. And I *do* love him."

"Pray, Katelyn. Just pray. But don't let this consume you. Right now you must focus on the people who need you. Understand?"

"Yes." Katelyn wanted to be able to focus on James, but her mother was right. She had other, more pressing matters with which to contend. Yet, she wasn't quite through. "Mama, with all my heart, I want to be with this man for the rest of my life. I'm just so very confused. I don't know which way to turn."

Mama touched Katelyn's shoulder. " 'Lean not on your own understanding. . .' "

That verse again. Katelyn had offered it to Martha, but she'd never expected the same thought might apply to her own situation. Katelyn had always thought she listened to God and yielded to His direction. But she obviously hadn't in this case.

It was so difficult to distinguish her own wants from her needs. A rush of emotions could be deafening. She had to trust in the Lord and not try to understand things that couldn't be understood for now. Surely, the Lord would reveal the answers. She'd just have to wait. It was God's timing, not her own.

Mama's voice interrupted Katelyn's thoughts. "You look so tired. Have you rested?"

"Haven't had time."

"You need to take care of yourself, or you won't be any good to anyone." She brushed a lock of wavy dark hair away from her clear green eyes. "Is somebody spelling you right now?"

"Yes. I just wanted to come and check on you, see you again."

Mama's gaze shifted to the freshly made bed. "Why don't you nap for a time? It'll do you good. I'll wake you a little later."

Bone-deep weariness had overcome Katelyn. Without a

word, she headed to the bed. She gratefully sank into the plush softness of the feather ticking.

"Here," said Mama. "Let me cover you with this." She gripped a folded patchwork quilt resting at the foot of the bed. Shaking it loose from its creases, she draped it over her daughter.

Clenching the blanket tight, Katelyn tugged it up around her shoulders. "Mama?" she whispered.

"What, sweetheart?"

"When will you be well enough to take over?" The fear of failure still had its talons in her.

A gentle smile caressed Mama's lips. "I won't be taking over, Katelyn."

"Why not? You're almost well. I've seen all the work you've done here."

"No. God planned this job for you. That's apparent."

"But I simply can't do it alone."

Mama held a section of quilt and rubbed at the stitching with her thumb. "You won't have to do it alone. I'll help."

"You'll help?" Katelyn's eyelids grew heavy despite herself.

"Of course," said her mother. "In a couple days I'll be strong enough to assist you. But I won't take over. You have to lead the way on this one."

Katelyn never heard her mother's last words. She had drifted into a sweet slumber. Nor did she see the tears her mother cried at her bedside, grateful that her two daughters had survived the disease that had taken her husband and son.

ten

James waved at Toby and Carrie as he dismounted. The two mimicked starlings, flapping their arms and making high-pitched screeching noises from deep inside tiny throats. He couldn't resist smiling. Children were truly a delight. They could always be expected to shed even the tiniest ray of light on the most hopeless situations.

After looping the reins around the post, he walked up the steps and opened the door. Before he even entered, he knew Katelyn was gone. The thought struck him as odd. A restlessness came over him.

Katelyn's nearness offered comfort. This was the first time he'd realized it. It was as though a pleasing glow surrounded her and caught up anybody near enough to benefit.

His brown gaze made note of the changes made in the interior of the soddie since he'd left. New cots had been set up against the wall nearest the door. Two women nursed the sick, while another hovered over a washboard, scrubbing laundry. A stack of freshly sewn sheets rested in the corner. An assortment of delectable food covered the table. Buckets of cool water sat near the hearth while more water boiled in the black iron kettle hanging directly over the flame.

Beth Jameston approached James. "Katelyn's gone," she said, as if she already knew what his question might be.

"Where?" James removed his hat and clenched it tight in his right fist.

"Poor soul needed a break," said Beth. "Might be she's home sleepin'."

"Yes," said James, "she needs some rest." He studied the cots until he found the one on which Martha lay in a mound of misery. She'd been moved closer to the others to make

99

room for the new cots. "I'll just see to Martha," he told Beth, dropping his gaze. Could it be so obvious that he missed Katelyn McKnight?

Clearing her throat, Beth told him, "Go right ahead. She's been callin' fer ya."

Calling for me? Compassion drove every step until he was at Martha's side. Then he was once again overtaken by confusion. At times, James felt like he was involved in some kind of practical joke and the joke was on him. His whole universe had turned inside out. What used to feel right, felt so wrong now. When would his world right itself?

Martha barely opened her eyes. Their blue depths were full of feverish heat. Tears spilled down her flushed cheeks. "J–James," she pleaded. "H–help me!"

He bent near her ear. "Shhh, I'm here, Martha."

"Don't feel good, James."

"I know you don't." He dabbed at her tears with the back of his index finger, worried the salt in them might sting the lesions forming on her face.

She tried to shift position but didn't have the strength. A weary cry caught in her throat from the effort.

James assisted her until she maneuvered herself to her side, facing him. "Is that better?" he asked, his voice taking the tone he would use on a child like Carrie or Toby.

She nodded. "Do. . .I have the pox, James?"

The question struck like a blow to the stomach. *How can I answer that? If I answer truthfully, will you give up the fight?* Drawing a deep breath, he spoke the truth. "Martha, yes, you've got the smallpox. But," he hurried, "you're gonna be fine. You're doing better than most. I can see it."

At first Martha didn't answer. A few more tears tried to find their way down her face. James wiped them away.

"How?" she finally asked.

"We were all exposed, Martha, the whole town." He thought for a moment. Something dawned on him. "Martha, remember your father's barn raising?"

"Uh huh."

"Practically everybody worked those three days. Remember?"

"Yes."

James knelt down on one knee to where he could study Martha eye to eye. "I think that's when we were all exposed. And then the dance came next. Some had already taken ill by then—my father included. And your little sister, Maggie," he added. "The Fontannas, the McKnights."

James watched as Martha's eyes closed. She slept. But his new understanding of how the epidemic had started raised one question: who had brought the disease to Cimarron? They might never know.

He stood quietly and wove his way to Maggie.

Her condition had not improved, but she wasn't any worse, either. James stepped past the other cots, studying their occupants briefly, wondering if he and some others should head out to bring more people to the Fontanna homestead for care.

This soddie was no longer considered off limits to the people in town. Instead all of Cimarron was quarantined. Telegraphs had been sent out to surrounding towns. The last shipments had been delivered. Cimarron would go it alone for a while. All James could do was hope for the best. Some things were out of his control.

Suddenly James caught sight of Beth Jameston dashing to the window. A rider had arrived. He didn't understand the urgency until Beth spoke.

"It's that Cheyenne squaw," she said, tension lacing her words. "She's got that babe of hers!"

James knew of the woman. A French trapper, named Chardoneau, had come to Cimarron when his wife was due to give birth. He'd married her among her people. They'd waited for the infant to grow stronger before engaging in their nomadic lifestyle again. There had been some complications with the baby at birth, but the tiny boy seemed to surmount his struggles.

Beth raced for the door just as the Indian woman entered, breathless and speaking a garble of unintelligible words.

James studied her as she spoke with animated gestures.

She was dressed in a shift of buffalo skin that reached down about halfway from the knee to her ankle. Two rows of blue beads ran across the front above the belt, which was ornamented with a fringe of hanging porcupine quills. Across her bare, left arm she wore two red painted stripes. A copper bracelet adorned her upper right arm. Her leggings, painted yellow, were fringed at the bottoms and along the sides. Horizontal black cross-lines wove their way around her legs.

The woman's long, shiny black hair was twisted into two braids with fringed rolls of deerskin tied to the outside of the braids. On the outer edge of the deerskin whirls, she'd fastened sprigs of sage as an additional ornament.

To James, seeing an Indian was like seeing a ghost. The Red River wars had consumed the Panhandle, with the army seeking to drive out the natives from the lands and allow white settlements to dot the vast plains from horizon to horizon.

Buffalo runners by the hundreds had nearly exterminated the buffalo, which provided life itself for the Indians. Shaking his head to clear his thoughts, James took a deep breath. He knew he had to focus on the issues at hand.

He watched as Beth grabbed the infant from his mother's arms and tugged down the soft deerhide covering to expose its tiny face. Her expression told the story.

The baby's mother grew frantic. In between words spoken in her Cheyenne tongue, James heard the word *seek* several times. She obviously knew little English, but he understood that she was trying to say *sick*.

"Where's your man?" Beth asked the woman, handing the child to one of the other women to begin his care.

The Indian woman shook her head, a desperate pleading expression shadowing large brown eyes.

"Chardoneau?" Beth tried. "Where's Chardoneau?"

James felt his heart slow its pace as understanding flickered on her brown face.

"Seek," she said, motioning with her hand toward town.

James knew what he must do. He slapped his hat on his head and stepped outside. "Cromwell! Flaggerty!" he called out. "Get the wagon. We have more people to fetch."

Without hesitation, they were off. James wished Katelyn would return.

≈

After a nap and a cup of sassafras tea, Katelyn made the journey back to the temporary hospital. Her mother supplied her with fresh herbs for tinctures, poultices, and ointments that should encourage relief of the smallpox symptoms.

Although she felt rested, Katelyn didn't relish the thought of returning. But her mother and James were right. God wouldn't have placed this on her shoulders if He didn't think she could handle the job. No, she wouldn't fail. Not if she tried her best. And that's what she intended to do.

Besides, she thought, as she crossed a ravine, *if I worry about failing, I won't be able to center my abilities where they are needed.*

Katelyn's attention was drawn to a beautiful black swallowtail butterfly that flitted among the delicate flowers of the shell-pink plains poppy mallow. She realized this was the first week of April. A warm breeze skirted her cheeks. Closing her eyes briefly, Katelyn allowed the gentle wind to caress her lashes.

Rounding a bend, she reached an open stretch of prairie brimming with new bunch grass, good grazing for the horses and cattle. Mock bishop's weed stretched its tiny white clusters of flowers across the silty soils, adding a delicate beauty to the land like a wash of dainty lace ribbing a plain bodice on a dress.

A certain peace settled into her, but it left just as quickly when she approached the Fontanna homestead. Squinting her eyes, Katelyn tried to understand the commotion at the front of the soddie. A wagon pulled up, driven by James, she recognized. Two men trailed on horseback. Beth Jameston peeked into the back of the wagon inquisitively.

A newcomer, Katelyn thought. She kicked the mule in the sides. She arrived at the wagon about the time James and the men were removing a man from the buckboard. Katelyn recognized him as the French trapper.

He was only supposed to be in town for a short time, she remembered, realizing how sad it was the small family had unwittingly gotten caught up in this Cimarron madness. Or unwittingly *brought* the madness. She hadn't considered that possibility.

"Such is the way of life," she said out loud, the sadness making her heart heavy with new despair. *Have faith,* she reminded herself.

The Cheyenne woman dashed outside at that moment and clung to her husband as they tried to move him into the soddie. Katelyn jumped off the mule, leaving the animal's reins to drag the ground. She raced to James's side.

Briefly, their eyes met. Just as quickly, their gazes turned to their duties and the people milling about them. Katelyn stepped to the Indian woman's side, wrapped a reassuring arm around her shoulders, and gently guided her off to the side. That freed the men to complete their task.

Beth made her way to Katelyn and the Cheyenne woman. "Am I glad to see you!" she said to Katelyn.

"Is everything okay?" Katelyn asked, concern etching lines into her forehead. The Cheyenne woman had grown quiet and no longer needed to be restrained. The three women quickly made their way into the soddie as Beth explained the latest events.

Katelyn left Beth to the woman and set plans in motion to care for the trapper.

The man was large—maybe two hundred fifty pounds of solid muscle. Long hair and the beard and mustache growth on his face made it difficult to view his skin and confirm everyone's fears. But when James removed the man's buckskin coat, his condition was all too clear.

"He's obviously been sick for some time," Katelyn told

James as she sponged water onto the trapper's face and throat. Beth handed her a ladle of cool water, but when Katelyn tried to feed it to him, the trapper nearly choked and spit it out.

"I won't be able to handle this one on my own," she warned James. "He's much too large, and he could get out of control."

"Don't worry," he told her, "whenever you need to deal with him, just call me. If I'm not here, one of the other men will help you." He hesitated. "Are you okay, Katelyn? Did you rest?"

"Yes, thank you," she told him, struggling to loosen the ties on the man's moccasins. James moved to her aid. Katelyn stepped aside, allowing him to complete the task. With him near, she realized, her despair seemed to melt away. It was as though she could handle anything as long as James was with her. She gave her mind a firm shake and tried to concentrate on her work, wondering if she would ever be able to give this worry about her feelings for James to God as well. It was so hard to let go.

Drawing a deep breath, she retrieved a muslin sheet and two gray wool army blankets. She draped these over the man, but he shrugged them off. He groaned and fought, mumbling all the while. Several times he struggled to lift himself off the cot, but James pushed him back down.

"Chardoneau," James said firmly. "You need to be still."

His efforts proved futile.

Katelyn gripped the blankets with one hand and rubbed at the tiny dip in her upper lip with her right pinky. She looked helplessly at James.

"He's out of control. I don't know how to help him."

James shook his head, an expression of concern covering his handsome features.

Again, Katelyn struggled to cover the brawny man with blankets, but he tugged them off once more. She moved closer, watched his breathing grow labored. His breaths were shallow, then retreated into spasms before becoming shallow once more. She knew.

"Try and keep him still, James. Talk to him if you can." She located Chardoneau's wife with her eyes and spoke to the woman without words. To her relief, the frightened woman stepped over to them.

Katelyn took the woman's tiny brown hand in her own pale fingers and gently massaged it. She looked deep into the woman's fear-filled brown eyes and shook her head. Then she drew her bottom lip in between her teeth, praying the Indian woman understood her meaning.

No tears fell as Chardoneau's wife stepped to her husband, bent low to his ear, and began whispering to him. His flailings grew weak. A gurgling sound marked each meager breath. Katelyn watched, tears brimming her lashes before splashing onto the woman's hand, still held in her own.

Seeking to find something to ease her pain, Katelyn found solace in James's eyes. They held a mixture of anticipation and sorrow. He managed a smile of reassurance, and Katelyn took it. When she drew her own deep breath, Chardoneau drew his last.

eleven

The town lost two more people after the trader's death: Gabe Appleburg and his wife, Whimsy. Their daughter Maggie still held on. For the moment, Katelyn decided against telling Martha about her losses, believing the news might make it that much harder for the young woman to fight her own battle against the deadly disease.

The cots of those who had died were filled within days with what Katelyn called newcomers. She refused to refer to them as sick any longer. A week passed. Katelyn spent much of her time not only tending the people, but singing to them as well. Her music made an obvious difference. The ballads seemed to take their minds off their agonies, if only for a short time. Some occasionally sang along, their voices weak, hoarse. Songs like "The Old Chisholm Trail" and "The Range of the Buffalo" filled the soddie. In a private moment, one of the patients told her that the community had nicknamed her the "Song of the Cimarron" because of her singing.

Katelyn discovered that in spite of sharing with her mother the gifts of a healer, she was her own person with her own way of working with people. She gained confidence and no longer feared failure. Her faith grew, leaving her with a calm peace about the future.

But there was one area that escaped this sense of peace. Whenever she thought of James, her mind flooded with questions. How would her feelings and his apparent commitment to Martha be reconciled? she wondered. She knew that she needed to trust her Lord in this matter, but Katelyn found that extremely difficult to actually do.

Then came the day when Katelyn's mother drove up in the buckboard. Carrie and Toby rode with her. Katelyn had been able to leave the children at home when her mother's strength had returned, but she was unspeakably relieved to know that her mother now felt well enough to offer support at the makeshift hospital. Except for a few scars on her mother's forehead and arms, Katelyn could see no tell-tale signs of the disease that nearly took the woman's life.

Days had passed since the most recent patients had been brought to the Fontanna site. Katelyn believed Cimarron was finally making its way out of the storm. Now she must concern herself with saving those hovering between life and death.

After Chardoneau's passing, his Indian wife became obviously depressed. She hovered in a corner most days, her hair hanging in her face, holding her sick infant son tight to her chest. She had sliced her arms with a knife, a Cheyenne custom of mourning, before they could wrestle the weapon away from her.

Many times during the course of a day, Katelyn stepped over to her, knelt down, and tried to offer comfort. She couldn't imagine how it must feel to be completely alone. The Cheyenne woman was here among strangers. She had lost her husband and would most likely lose her child. Katelyn couldn't fathom how great the woman's misery must be. Many times Katelyn had cried for the young woman, feeling frustrated by her own inability to help.

Sometimes the young mother tried to communicate. She said, *"Tsis tsis tas,"* over and over with a pleading expression straining her thinning brown features. Beth thought she spoke of her people. Katelyn agreed. That's what she, herself, would desire if she were in the other woman's position. She'd want to be home again.

"We have to watch her," she warned James as they ate lunch together.

"Why?"

"We can't let her leave. She'll go straight to her people. I know it, James. And then she'll expose them all."

"That, on top of what the army's already doing to them," James said, regret filling his voice.

Katelyn understood his feelings about the issue. But there was little they could do on a large scale. Their focus had to be on preventing yet another tragedy from happening to the Cheyenne. Glancing the woman's way, Katelyn watched her mother retrieve the infant from the Cheyenne woman and care for him. Nobody knew the Cheyenne girl's name. Katelyn decided to call her Mrs. Chardoneau. After all, she was a person like them and deserved respect.

Turning back to James, she asked, "Will you help me watch her?"

"I'll do it," said James. He took a bite of corn pone, followed by a gulp of fresh cow's milk.

Katelyn's mother approached them, the baby nestled in her arms. Katelyn studied the bundle, then noticed the intense concern in her mother's green eyes. She stole another glance at the newborn, then back to her mother. James set his spoon down with a clank, obviously sensing something amiss.

"What is it, Mother?" Katelyn questioned. "What's wrong?"

Drawing a deep breath, her mother replied, "He's gone."

"The baby?"

"Yes, dear. The little one's with the Lord now."

"Does Mrs. Chardoneau know?" James asked.

"Don't think so."

Katelyn's shoulders grew heavy. *Who will tell her? How will she respond when she finds out?*

As though hearing her thoughts, Katelyn's mother said, "I think the little boy passed on a few hours back, and for some reason, she doesn't know—or doesn't want to accept it."

"Goodness," said Katelyn. "If she does realize, she might steal off to her people."

"My concern, too," her mother agreed. "To make matters worse, I think Mrs. Chardoneau is running a fever. She doesn't look right."

At that moment, the young mother made her way to them

and reclaimed her infant son, clutching him tightly. She returned to the corner without a backward glance.

Katelyn watched. The woman never checked her baby. She just held him. Suddenly it struck Katelyn that she hadn't seen Mrs. Chardoneau nurse the child all day. The woman had to know! But somehow, her mind refused to accept the fate of the child. Obviously she was still in shock over the loss of her husband. How could she handle yet another tragedy?

"I say we leave her be for now," said James, glancing the woman's way. He peered back at Katelyn, his brown eyes questioning. "Your call."

"I agree. What do you think, Mama?"

"I think James is right. I'll let the others know the situation. Maybe by sunup we can come up with a solution."

Both Katelyn and James nodded in agreement. Katelyn had lost her appetite and shoved the tin of food away. James did the same. Katelyn's mother spun on her heel to leave but turned back just as quickly to face her daughter again.

Leaning in close, she whispered, "You might see what you can do for Martha. Seems she's having a hard time of it. Poor thing is fretful about the spots on her face."

Rising, Katelyn smoothed her cream-colored muslin skirts and stepped away from the bench. "I'll go to her."

Katelyn walked over to Martha's cot and sat down on the edge of it. "What is it, Martha?" she asked.

Martha could only manage a hoarse, raspy cry. Blue eyes gazed out from beneath puffy lids. No tears flowed. She had been treated with water, medicinal tea, and ointment. Still, to Katelyn, she looked bad, very bad.

Concern edged Katelyn's voice. "What do you need?"

"These sores," Martha croaked. "They're all over my face."

"It'll be okay," Katelyn reassured. "We're taking care of them."

"No," argued Martha, with what little strength she had. "They're going to scar me. I know it. I—I've seen it."

Katelyn didn't know how to respond. She tried putting

herself in Martha's position. It wasn't hard. Hadn't there been times when she herself had worried about not being beautiful? She remembered the words her mother had so patiently imparted. Now it was time to pass on the lesson to someone who needed it.

"Martha," Katelyn said softly. "True beauty comes from inside a person. Don't you know that?" She waited. Martha didn't respond, though she still watched Katelyn. *How can I get through to you,* Katelyn wondered, *when you've been beautiful all your life?* It had been hard enough for Katelyn to come to grips with her appearance; it must be doubly so for this woman.

She tried again. "Martha, listen to me. You've got a wonderful life ahead of you. You're going to have beautiful children with—" She stopped abruptly. Swallowing her feelings, Katelyn continued.

"You're going to do wonderful things, accomplish great goals, meet challenges!" She hesitated. "You're a strong woman, Martha." Her eyes filled with tears of understanding. "And. . .and you are still beautiful."

For a time, Martha just stared straight ahead. When she finally spoke, her words brought hope to Katelyn's heart, hope that an awakening might be occurring in Martha.

"I–I'm so sorry I've been mean to you, Katelyn. I've been so mean to everyone. Now look at me. I'm being punished."

"No, no, Martha, that's not true. Our Lord is a loving, merciful Lord. You're not being punished. You just got sick is all."

"But. . .you haven't. Why?"

Katelyn explained the cowpox to Martha. "Besides," she added, "you're not the only one sick here. Many are suffering. God didn't single you out, no more than He did anybody else."

Martha reached up and rubbed at a developing sore above her left eyebrow. "I'm sleepy," she said, "very sleepy."

"Then, you just go ahead and rest."

"Will you stay with me?"

"Of course, Martha. As long as you need."

❧

James sat at the table, overhearing Katelyn's conversation with Martha. As he heard Katelyn's last words, his heart ached. Katelyn was a precious gem. Her compassion stretched farther than any person's he'd ever known.

How could she show so much care and sympathy to a person who'd behaved in a mean and selfish way to everybody around her? Even as he asked himself the question, James knew the answer. Katelyn couldn't be any other way. She loved people, cared for them. She could never carry anger for long, never hold a grudge. People like her were rare. They simply lived to love others, just as God did.

Massaging his left temple, James rose from the table. There was work to be done at several of the places in town. People needed livestock tended, chores completed.

Making his way out onto the front porch, he sat down on the step for a minute to gather his thoughts. Knowing he loved Katelyn McKnight with all his heart, he felt helpless to control that love. He certainly couldn't stop it. The thing materialized of its own will, though he tried to deny it. Remembering his prayer, he realized nothing had changed. And he felt powerless to change the situation himself.

James stood abruptly, slapped his Stetson against his right thigh, and trudged the distance to his horse.

Okay, he thought, *if it can't be changed, I'd better accept it.* Yet he could never deny his love for Katelyn. It had blossomed into a full, glorious thing. He'd fought it only to discover that he couldn't battle something stronger than himself. Love. How could God have allowed this to happen? Was he being punished somehow?

Katelyn's words rushed back to him like floodwaters. *Our God is a loving, merciful God.* Yes, it was true. He'd seen the evidence all around him. But why was all this happening? And why hadn't the Lord answered his prayers?

Gripping the reins that hung down from the horse's mouth,

James swung them over the animal's broad head. He slipped his left foot in the stirrup, swung his right leg over the animal's back, and landed gently in the saddle. Slapping the leather straps against the paint's thick neck, James set off toward town. Work might take his mind off things. But he doubted it.

❧

Katelyn softly called Martha's name. The woman did not stir. Quietly Katelyn got up from the edge of the cot and stepped away, careful not to wake the woman.

Katelyn's mother had kept busy sponging the patients down with cool water, attempting to bring down the stubborn fevers. She approached Katelyn.

"How'd it go with Martha?"

"I think it went okay. I mean, she said something I've never heard her say."

"What?" Katelyn's mother set her bowl of water down on the puncheon floor.

"Sorry. She said *sorry."*

For a moment, neither spoke. Then Katelyn's mother said, "That's a good start for the girl, to say *sorry."*

Katelyn smiled. "I told her what you told me when I felt the same way. Remember?"

Her mother returned Katelyn's smile, reached out, and gave her daughter's hand a liberal squeeze. "What needs done next?" she questioned, changing the subject. A few feverish moans drifted through the air.

"I boiled some sassafras tea earlier. We need to get a dose into each person—as much as they can take."

"I'll get right on it." Katelyn's mother paused. "Maybe tonight will be quieter than the others so we all can get some rest."

"I certainly hope so, Mother. Would be nice to sleep through an entire night."

With another smile, Katelyn's mother moved on to her tasks.

Katelyn glanced around the room, searching for James. When she couldn't locate him, she stepped to the window. Then she moved outside. She heard the clanking of hammers and lifted her gaze to the roof. One man attached a section of thin board over a small leak so rain wouldn't seep into the house. Another unhitched horses from the buckboard and began feeding the mules, the milk cow, and all the horses on the property buckets of oats. James was nowhere in sight.

Katelyn's forehead wrinkled into the bridge of her nose. She drew her bottom lip in between her teeth. This was not like James. He *always* let her know where he was going. Something must be wrong! The very thought unnerved her. He hadn't seemed right all day. She wondered if he was feeling the death of his father more intensely. And she wasn't there to comfort him.

Peering back at the soddie, Katelyn knew everybody was being taken care of. She tossed her green gaze toward the mule she rode in on and saw Flaggerty start to unsaddle the creature.

Trailing dry prairie dust, Katelyn raced to him, her skirts flying behind. "Stop!" she sputtered breathlessly. "I'll be needing that mule for a while. Can you leave the saddle on? Please?"

" 'Course, ma'am. Glad to oblige ya." He tugged on the strap to tighten the saddle, then handed the reins over to Katelyn. The man walked away to pursue other duties.

I won't be long, she thought. *I just need to find James, make sure he's all right.* Katelyn jumped on the mule's back and kicked the animal lightly in the sides. "Get on!" she hastened, turning the beast in the direction of Cimarron. The day had sped by, Katelyn thought wearily, as she viewed the setting sun. Before long, she rode into the wide dirt road of Cimarron and studied the wood sidewalks and sign boards lining the streets, enticing customers to businesses.

Keeping the mule at a slow trot, she made her way to the mercantile. No lamps were lit. She turned the mule around and headed back the other way. The only glow of light came from the livery stable owned by John Dorman. He, too, had suffered blows from the smallpox epidemic.

As she drew nearer, she caught sight of James's paint stabled outside. *What would he be doing here?* she mused. Quietly she slipped off the mule, tied him next to the paint, and started to make her way inside.

The sounds of voices stopped her. She moved closer to the door and peeked inside, not wishing to interrupt anything. A kerosene lamp cast light over the stalls, which housed several quiet horses. She caught sight of the men apparently in deep conversation.

Suddenly Katelyn felt like an intruder. She twirled around to make her departure. James's words stopped her cold, as if a pail of icy water had been tossed in her face.

"I didn't know love would be this way," he confided to his friend.

"That's the way of love, young fella," answered John, sorting through a pile of horseshoes.

"Was it this miserable for you the first time you fell in love?"

"Ah," said John, squaring his shoulders at James. "Was both miserable and confusin'. Weren't prepared any better'n you. The woman filled my head day and night. Found it hard to work, to eat, to sleep."

"Yeah, that's the feeling," James agreed, holding his hand above the heat rising from the top of the lantern.

"Who's got yer heart, fella? If ya don't mind my askin'."

Katelyn felt her own heart race inside her chest. This was the moment of truth, when she would discover whom James loved. *Martha,* she told herself, trying to accept that fact so she wouldn't be forever crushed when James admitted the truth.

Tears filled her eyes. Then he spoke. Katelyn fought hard to contain herself.

twelve

"Katelyn McKnight," James answered with only the slightest hesitation.

Katelyn couldn't believe her ears. Beads of sweat formed around her hairline, despite the chilly night. Her legs trembled. She had to lean against the rough outer wood plank wall of the building for support.

"Katelyn McKnight, Katelyn McKnight." She mouthed the name several times, enjoying the feel of it on her lips, loving the sound when James spoke it.

He loves me, she thought, *as I love him.* Her mother had been right all along. John's words interrupted her reverie.

"Fine woman, that Katelyn McKnight. Fine woman indeed. And talented I hear," he added.

"Not one finer," James affirmed, "probably in all the world. And I just happened to find her in the little town of Cimarron."

John chuckled. "You're smitten, that's fer sure." He worked to control his amusement. "I hear tell folks have labeled that Katelyn McKnight as the Song of the Cimarron."

"I've heard that, too." James shifted his weight from foot to foot. "She has a beautiful voice, John, absolutely lovely."

"Well, whatcha gonna do now, fella?"

James paused.

Katelyn waited impatiently.

"Don't know for certain," James finally answered. "I'm having some other problems, too."

"Comes with the territory," said John, chuckling again. "Glad I done got through it. Made me miserable awful for a long spell."

Quietly, Katelyn slipped back to the mule and retrieved the

reins. As she headed toward home, she wondered what James had meant by "other problems." Must be the mercantile. With his father gone, the business now rested entirely on James's shoulders. Yes, she reasoned, that must be it.

The ride back out to the Fontanna place was a peaceful journey for Katelyn, despite the site of a raccoon and her babies dashing for cover, a porcupine nearly running beneath her mule's hooves, and a skunk edging close enough to spray.

The sounds of crickets and prairie owls created a symphony in the night air. Thickets moved as silent occupants settled down for the night. But Katelyn hadn't a care in the world. To her, everything seemed different, so incredibly ideal.

She dropped down into a ravine, then guided the mule over a low bluff, the beast moving effortlessly. By the time she reached the homestead, darkness fully engulfed the tiny sod home. A few candles remained lit in case somebody needed emergency attention during the night. A lard oil lamp glowed on the table at a low pitch.

Katelyn managed to unsaddle the mule, remove its harness and bit, and stable him for the night. Fumbling around in the inky blackness, she succeeded in tossing a pile of oats on the ground for him to eat, then made her way to the house. Everybody slept—everyone except Martha.

All the helpers had gone home for the day, leaving Katelyn's mother, Toby, and Carrie. The two children lay on pallets. Katelyn's mother rested in the slat-backed rocker she'd brought from home, reading the Bible by what little light a nearby candle provided.

Glancing expectantly at Martha, then back again to her mother, Katelyn asked, "What's wrong with her?"

Her mother rested the well-worn Bible in her lap, folded her hands on top of the volume, and looked up at her daughter. "Poor thing has fretted since you left. Where'd you steal off to? Was a mite worried, child."

"I'm sorry, Mama." Clearing her throat, Katelyn explained, "I couldn't find James and grew concerned. I knew everything was taken care of here, so I went searching."

Her mother smiled. Katelyn relaxed, but only temporarily. Martha began whimpering.

"Katelyn? That you?" Martha's weak voice was high with panic.

Katelyn wanted more than anything to share her news with her mother, but this was not the time. Martha needed her. Just before she reached Martha, a new thought surfaced. "How's Mrs. Chardoneau?" she whispered over to her mother.

"Not well," the woman answered, standing up and placing her Bible on the rocker's worn seat. "She's in the same corner, curled into a ball. Won't let anybody touch that babe of hers."

"Umm." Katelyn glanced toward the corner, but darkness prevented her from viewing the poor woman.

"Wonder if we can get her into a cot tomorrow," Katelyn said more to herself.

"All's we can do is try," her mother answered. "But she's a stubborn girl, so it won't be an easy task."

That was true. It wouldn't be easy to do much of anything with the woman. She was as frightened as an injured animal. "I'm going to go see what I can do for Martha," Katelyn said, worry still permeating her mind for Mrs. Chardoneau.

Katelyn's mother loosened the pins holding her hair in a bun. The long strands fell about her shoulders and down her back in silky cascades. Katelyn loved the look and feel of her mother's hair. It was even longer than her own. A delicate hint of gray touched its chestnut coloring, adding to its glossy sheen.

"I'm going to check foreheads," Katelyn's mother said, "see if anybody needs sponging."

"Good, that's very good."

Without another word, the two went their separate ways.

When Katelyn reached Martha, soft sobs rose in the woman's chest, escaping from between chapped lips.

Candlelight glanced off the few tears glistening on her cheeks.

Martha caught sight of Katelyn and reached out an arm, extending fingers of need. "Why did you leave me?" Her voice squeaked, sounding like a frightened child. "You said you wouldn't leave me!"

Katelyn bent over the girl and massaged blond curls back off her forehead. The lesions covering her face and extremities had begun to form crusty scabs. She was careful not to rub off any of these, lest they become aggravated and bleed.

"Shh," Katelyn soothed, "I'm here now, right here."

"Why did you leave me?" Martha's face formed a pain-stricken grimace as tears continued to forge silvery paths down her pale features, colored only by fevered cheeks.

Sitting down on the edge of the cot, near Martha's head, Katelyn explained, "I had to help the others after you fell asleep. Is that okay? That I helped the others?"

Martha nodded, and the tears ceased. "They need you, too."

Surprise welled inside Katelyn, and she didn't know how to respond. Finally she said, "Yes, that's right, Martha. The others need me, too."

Reaching out a hand, Katelyn gripped Martha's fingers in her own. They felt hot, but not as hot as before. And unlike her sister Maggie, Martha never lost her reason. That was an excellent sign.

"Where's my mama?" Martha asked unexpectedly. "I need my mama."

Katelyn placed a hand to her chest in an attempt to steady her racing heart and forced herself to breathe. What should she do? What should she tell Martha?

"I've been looking for them," Martha said, interrupting Katelyn's thoughts. "All I see is Maggie."

"Well. . .uh. . ." Katelyn struggled with the words. Suddenly she realized what she must do. She should tell Martha the truth and pray for the best.

"Where are they?" Martha asked again. "Please tell me!"

"Okay," Katelyn managed. She cleared her throat. "Maggie's doing real well, Martha. Your baby sister is truly a fighter."

"I know. She's always been the stronger of the two of us. But where are my folks?"

Katelyn studied Martha for a moment, agonizing over the anxiety that shone from the young woman's blue eyes. "Martha, the truth is. . .they're no longer here."

"Did you move them? Someplace else? Are they back home being cared for by Carlos and Mandy?"

Tears of frustration formed in Katelyn's eyes, but she didn't dare reach up to dash them away.

"No, Martha." Her voice softened considerably. "They're gone." She hesitated when she saw Martha's mouth drop open. "They've gone to be with the Lord," she finished.

Martha's shocked expression remained fixed for several seconds, as though her face had been carved from stone. Then tiny sobs escaped, followed by larger ones, until finally her entire body shook with uncontrollable spasms.

Katelyn drew Martha into her arms and held her snug, allowing her to cry into her shoulder, trying to steady her trembling form by squeezing tighter.

Maybe a half hour elapsed, Katelyn wasn't sure, before she felt Martha's body go limp. The poor woman had cried herself to sleep.

"Good, Martha, that's very good," she whispered, as she rested the young woman's body back on the cot. Gently, Katelyn covered Martha from head to toe with sheets and quilts, tucking blankets in under her feet and around the sides of her body.

Walking softly amid the cots, Katelyn located the rocker, lifted the Bible off the seat, and settled her weary body down in the chair. A few of the muscles in her back trembled involuntarily before relaxing. Although an intense edge of weariness cast its shadow over Katelyn, she managed a brief prayer for Martha, for them all. Then she thumbed through the pages of the book.

Opening to the book of Exodus, Katelyn ran her finger down the columns until she came to the twenty-fifth verse of the twenty-third chapter. She had no idea why she'd stopped there. She began to read the words silently: *So you shall serve the Lord your God, and He will bless your bread and your water. And I will take sickness away from the midst of you.*

With that promise resting on her heart, Katelyn fell asleep, the Bible still open on her lap.

≥

James returned and found his usual place on the porch for catching a few winks. He couldn't find sleep right away. A flood of thoughts overwhelmed his mind, making him downright irritable. Martha steadily improved, and he was relieved to see that. The town had lost enough people already. As soon as Martha was over the worst of the smallpox, James knew what he must do. The thought caused him to jerk wide awake. He tried to settle back again and put the Stetson over his face, hoping that might aid his quest for sleep. Next images of Katelyn filled his thoughts.

His lips tightened into two white lines, and he sat up abruptly. He wished his father were here. James needed desperately to explain things to him. He knew once he understood, his father would never require James to marry Martha Appleburg.

No, he hadn't courted Katelyn as was customary. *What does that matter?* he wanted to shout. *If a person knew he was in love, then customs were only followed for tradition's sake.* A new thought struck him.

Do you love me, Katelyn? Why hadn't he thought of that before? Did he just expect this to be a one-sided effort? Of course not, he reasoned. But he had been so involved in his own emotions that he never considered her feelings. A union wasn't formed until both people loved each other unconditionally.

"Ohh," James groaned. He tried to rehash the time he'd spent with Katelyn, tried to find some reason to believe she loved him. His mind traveled back to the time he first set eyes on Katelyn, just after finding Toby. At that point, there was fear in her heart, pure fear. He saw no return of his feelings for her in her eyes. Quickly he scanned his memory. Worry had filled her eyes when she learned of Doc Hanson's fall. Other times, all he witnessed was her desire to work hard and her fear of failure.

James's heart felt like a lead weight hanging in his chest. Katelyn might not have any feelings toward him other than friendship. He had seen nothing to tell him otherwise. James silently rebuked himself for the shape his future was taking because of his earlier mistakes. He had been having fun, had not taken much time for serious planning. Now he knew that he should have. It wouldn't have been difficult to care for those around him and not just for himself. But no. He'd had to consume himself with worldly pleasures and thoughts.

Realizing he'd learned his lesson too late, James sighed with anger, anger at himself. Leaning back, he tugged the Stetson over his face. Maybe this was for the best, he reasoned. He hadn't forgotten about Martha, knew what was to come. It would be easier for Katelyn McKnight if she never thought of him as other than a friend. If she did ever grow to love him, how would she handle his impending proposal to Martha? That would not go well.

It was best that this love remain one-sided, James reasoned. It would be his suffering and his alone. He would never wish this kind of agony on Katelyn. His heart might never heal, but at least Katelyn could be spared unnecessary pain.

James drifted off to sleep.

thirteen

Somebody touched her shoulder. Opening her eyes, Katelyn saw her mother smiling down on her, one hand behind her back as though hiding something.

"Everyone made it through the night," Mother announced.

Katelyn extended both arms over her head and arched her body with the relief the stretch brought. "That's wonderful news!" She paused. "Did you sleep?"

"Laid down beside Carrie. Had a nice rest."

"Good, that's. . ." Katelyn stopped, then giggled, slipping one hand over her mouth.

"Very good," her mother completed.

Rising, Katelyn threaded fingers through her tangle of hair, making it more presentable. Then she smoothed her cream-colored skirts with both palms. "Ugh," she groaned. "Wish I could change into a fresh dress."

At that moment, her mother brought out the item she'd been hiding.

A wide smile stretched across Katelyn's face. She took the fresh pink and brown check gingham dress with leg-o'-mutton puffed sleeves and shook out its folds. Placing the material to her nose, Katelyn breathed in the scent of home. An aroma of sage mingled with lye soap delighted her senses.

"If you hurry," her mother suggested, "you can change before they start waking up."

Katelyn studied her mother for a moment. The woman was dressed in green percale. Her hair had been brushed and twisted up into a loose bun. She looked happy, truly happy, for the first time in nearly a month.

"Mama," she quizzed, "can I ask you something?"

"You know you can."

Katelyn draped the dress over the back of the rocker as she faced the woman. "Are you okay? I mean. . .really okay?"

"I miss your pa and little Jacob," she answered, tears threatening to spill onto her cheeks. "Always will. But they're with the Lord now. They're happy. I know they are."

Katelyn asked, "How did you get through it so effortlessly?" She remembered James's tears and Martha's agonizing cries.

"Don't think it was easy," her mother stated. "Fact is, it was the hardest thing for me to handle in my life." She rested a hand on the rocker as though supporting herself. "You see, Katelyn, even though I was sick, I knew I'd lost them. I mourned then. There were times I didn't think I'd pull through, didn't think I wanted to pull through."

"I'm so sorry, Mama. I didn't know."

Her mother gave Katelyn a slight smile. A tear slipped from her eye. She paused, massaged the back of her neck. "I knew when I lost them, knew it in my heart. And then you— I knew the agony you were going through, having to bury them, worrying over me and Carrie. But I was helpless to help you."

Katelyn moved closer to her, peering intensely into her mother's green eyes, eyes so like her own. "I can't imagine what that must have felt like, being so very ill on top of grieving." Yet her mother made it through. In that moment, Katelyn found hope for Martha. The young woman would grieve now, too, but she could still survive. "At least I wasn't sick."

"No, sweetheart," her mother answered, "but your experience was not easier than my own—just different."

"Yes, I suppose that's true."

Mother continued. "Then when you left and came to the Fontanna place, I cried and cried." She looked away briefly, gazing at Carrie, who still slept on the pallet next to Toby. She studied Katelyn again.

"I had to go on, Daughter, for you and Carrie. God had more work for me to do here on earth. My time will come to go be with your pa again, but not now." She faltered, swallowed hard, then continued.

"You must know, Katelyn, that I'm still mourning my loss and will most likely continue to grieve to some extent 'til I go to be with the Lord. I'll have good days and bad. Soon as things settle down, I imagine you'll see more of those bad days."

"That's okay," Katelyn whispered, "we'll get through those bad days together."

"Now," said her mother with a flick of her wrist, "better see to getting into that clean dress, or you won't have time before long."

Nodding, Katelyn wrapped her arms around the tiny woman and placed her cheek next to her mother's ear. "I love you."

Without another word, she gripped the dress and slipped into the kitchen lean-to. Katelyn gave herself a quick sponging off with some of the water left over that night. She dressed in the crisp pink and brown check gingham.

After slipping on her black lace-up boots, she brushed her hair until it shone. Gripping the now-empty pail, she reentered the room to see her mother busily feeding a few of the newcomers.

Toby and Carrie woke at the same time. Katelyn washed their faces and handed them each a couple corn pones, then sent them outside with quick hugs.

They dashed outside, only to run back in, squealing with delight. Katelyn saw they were spattered with raindrops. She settled them down with a couple toys and stepped to the front door.

Opening it, she scanned a blustery sky. Winds had picked up over the night, and a light drizzle misted the prairie landscape. She heard a noise to her left. James.

He'd obviously heard the door open and now rose to his feet, gripping his Stetson in one hand while raking through his tangle of black hair with the other.

The smile Katelyn threw him was wide, too wide for her

liking, so she quickly toned it down. To her dismay, James didn't return the smile. He slapped his hat against one muscled thigh. "Mornin'," he mumbled, hardly glancing at Katelyn.

What's wrong with you? "Are you hungry?" she asked, trying to maintain her composure.

"Could eat something, I guess. Not real hungry, though."

She wanted to question him on his changed mood but decided not to. Maybe later that afternoon, when everybody slept, they'd have a better chance of uninterrupted conversation.

His words she'd heard the night before passed through her mind: *I have other problems, too.* Katelyn wanted to help James with whatever bothered him, but she wasn't sure how to approach the issue. She'd think on it the better part of the day, pray on it.

Nodding, she turned and entered the door to the soddie, James trailing her.

"I'm going to get fresh water, first," James said, "then I'll come in and eat."

Katelyn watched him retrieve three pails and move to his task. When he returned, she poured the contents of one vessel into the iron kettle for brewing tea. James stoked the fire, adding buffalo chips, dry twisted grass, and discarded lumber scraps left over from making cots.

A warmth spread over them as the fire blazed. People shifted on their cots, waking. Katelyn retrieved a few tumblers, filled them with cool water, and delivered the drinks to thirsty patients.

She had to force the fluid down Maggie. The girl hadn't improved. To Katelyn, she seemed worse. Her fever had fired up in the night, flushing her cheeks, causing her blue-gray eyes to gloss over. Nor did she move much.

Katelyn heard Martha calling her name. She went to her, offering a cup of water. Martha downed the liquid in one gulp and asked for more. Katelyn obliged her, relieved the woman looked so well this morning. As Martha sipped the second cup, Katelyn studied her.

"How are you feeling?"

"Much better, thank you."

The eruptions on her face, arms, and legs still presented a problem, but Martha carried no signs of fever.

"Can you eat something?"

Martha nodded.

Katelyn retrieved a biscuit and handed it to Martha, who took ginger bites but managed to swallow what she put into her mouth.

"How's my sister?" Martha asked.

Again, the woman astonished Katelyn. Martha had never before voiced concern for someone other than herself. Now she asked after her sister. Wishing only to be truthful, Katelyn replied, "She seems to be doing a little worse today, Martha."

Martha didn't answer. She gazed in the direction of her sister's cot. The points of her blond brows met in the middle of her forehead.

"I'm sure she'll be okay," Katelyn hurriedly reassured, not wanting to unnecessarily upset Martha.

Turning her attention on Katelyn again, Martha said, "But, she's the strongest of both of us. Always has been."

"Maybe stronger in some ways. We all have our strengths and our weaknesses."

"Yes," Martha murmured, studying her sister again. Her bottom lip trembled.

"It'll be all right, Martha. I'm sure Maggie will be just fine," Katelyn consoled.

Tears swelled in her eyes. "She's all I have left," Martha confided. "I need my sister."

Katelyn understood that need. She had lost family members but was blessed to have her mother and baby sister still with her. If Martha lost Maggie, she would have nobody except distant relatives to lay claim to.

The seriousness of Martha's situation suddenly dawned on Katelyn. Martha, as the eldest surviving daughter, was now heir to her father's estate. Did she know anything about running a bank? Or a burgeoning cattle empire? Martha stood to inherit wealth she couldn't possibly handle, having paid little attention to the details of running either business while her father was alive.

Katelyn also knew Martha might lose the bank. People would be wanting their money once they learned that Gabe Appleburg had died. Many men in town wouldn't want to keep their finances in Martha's inexperienced hands. The situation appeared grim for both Martha and Maggie.

Pulling her attention back to Martha, Katelyn advised, "Just pray and believe with all your heart that Maggie will pull through."

Tugging the blankets up around her shoulders, Martha responded, "Maybe you should pray, Katelyn. God answers your prayers."

"The Lord hears all our prayers, Martha."

"No, but I mean. . .I haven't been half the Christian you've been." She pulled at a limp blond ringlet. "I don't think my faith is as strong as yours."

Katelyn smiled. "Then start now and make your faith strong." She gripped the empty cup Martha handed back to her. "It's never too late, Martha."

"I just don't think—"

"Let me tell you something," Katelyn interrupted. "When this smallpox epidemic began, I, too, didn't have the faith I should have had."

"You?" Martha's eyes flashed with astonishment.

"Yes, me." Katelyn paused. "I was afraid, especially when the doctor died. I didn't know if I could handle all this. But I prayed and prayed, Martha, asking the Lord to give me strength and direction. He did. Now you must do the same. Just believe when you pray, and He will answer—not always with the answer we want, but with what's best for us. That's where faith comes in. You believe and that's your faith. If you doubt, faith cannot take root. Don't doubt. And accept whatever answer He provides."

For a long time, neither said a word. Then, Martha spoke, her voice tremulous. "Do you really think I can have a faith like yours?"

"Martha, you can have a faith the size of a mustard seed, and wonderful things will happen." She reached out and touched Martha's hand. "Don't look to anybody else. Just keep your eyes on the Father, and He will direct your paths."

"Will you at least help me?" Martha asked suddenly.

"Of course, I will help you. But remember, nobody can have faith for you. It takes work, Martha, for all of us, and we must each find the way on our own."

Martha drew a deep breath. "I've got a long way to go," she admitted. "I know that. I still find myself struggling with selfish thoughts."

"It'll take some time, Martha. Most conversions don't happen overnight. Just be patient with yourself as the changes begin to take place—and they will take place."

"But how can I get these selfish thoughts to go away?"

Considering her words, Katelyn finally responded. "When I feel a certain way, a way I know is wrong, I react another way."

"What do you mean?"

"For instance, you might suddenly be overcome with a desire to have something, a new dress perhaps. Do just the opposite of what you feel. Give a dress away to somebody who really needs it. The new habits will soon overcome the bad ones."

Understanding filled Martha's eyes. There was a long moment of silence, then Martha spoke. "Okay. I'm ready."

"Ready?" Confusion settled on Katelyn's face.

"To pray." Martha gripped Katelyn's hand. "Let's pray."

Katelyn bowed her head and closed her eyes. The two women prayed. A sense of joy filled Katelyn's heart at Martha's new understanding and at her acceptance of her new role in life. *Thank you, Father,* Katelyn prayed silently as the words ceased and an *Amen* echoed in her ears.

❧

James struggled to eat the apple pie, knowing he'd need nourishment to get through the day. Martha had improved dramatically. He would have to propose soon. Right now he thought he'd head to the mercantile and unload the last shipment that came in and try to establish a business routine again.

Things had settled down for Cimarron. James was worried about Maggie, though. She'd taken a turn for the worse. He wondered if she'd pull through or not. At least Martha and the others were on the way back to health.

He'd watched Katelyn perform her duties, had seen her praying with Martha. It hurt to watch, knowing what he must do. He ached with love for the woman but could only love her from afar.

Rising from the table, James scooted the plate back and gripped his hat. His eyes were drawn to where Katelyn worked on the other side of the room. With long strides, James made his way to her.

Katelyn was sponging Maggie's forehead and neck. The young girl cried fitfully, fighting the procedure. With calm assurance and comforting words, Katelyn continued until the task was complete.

I love you, Katelyn, he wanted to say. Instead he told her where he was headed.

Katelyn looked up at him. "How long will you be?" she asked.

"Don't know." James stepped closer to her. He wanted to breathe of her scent, have something of Katelyn to take with him.

"I have to unload some supplies," he added, looking down at her, studying her features, wanting to remember them, wanting to burn everything about Katelyn McKnight into his memory to store for a lifetime. It was all he would have of his true love: memories. The thought stirred his anger again, and he shifted his weight from one foot to the other.

Not caring, James reached out and touched Katelyn's shoulder, gently, briefly, but with more in the touch than would normally be present.

Katelyn studied his eyes. "I guess I'll see you when you get back," she told him, a smile sweetening her face.

"Anything you want me to bring back from the mercantile?"

Thinking, Katelyn finally answered, "Not that I can think of, for now."

He placed his hat securely on his head as though trapping the anger beneath it. "I'll be back soon, then," he stated with forced detachment. Without another word, James left.

Neither James nor Katelyn saw Martha watching them, tears running in streams down her cheeks.

fourteen

"What's troubling you?" Katelyn's mother asked her on her way to retrieve a fresh nightshirt for one of the newcomers.

Katelyn didn't realize she wore her concern on her face. "I'm worried about James," she answered, straining the sassafras tea through a section of cheesecloth. She threw sprigs of mint into the boiling tea water for taste and would add honey to sweeten it later.

Just then Carrie ran up to her mother, tugging on her percale skirts. "Want some pudding," she pleaded in her child-like voice.

"What do you say?" her mother corrected.

"Pwease."

The woman smiled at her little girl. Toby looked on from his place near the door, where he held his toy soldier.

"Why don't you go back and play," she answered. "I'll get you both some pudding in a few minutes. Okay?"

Without a word, Carrie raced back to her playmate, telling him with animated gestures they would soon get a treat.

"What are you worried about?" Katelyn's mother turned her attention back to her older daughter.

Katelyn stopped working and faced her mother. She held the dripping cheesecloth in her fingers, allowing it to drain over the pail. "Something's bothering him, Mama, and I'm not sure what it is."

"Maybe he's just tired. We all are, you know."

"That's not it." Katelyn drew a deep breath. "I overheard something," she confessed. Quickly, she explained what transpired the night before when she went to look for James.

"That's wonderful!" her mother exclaimed. "Not that you eavesdropped, but that you have your answer." Her smile told how delighted she was with the news.

But Katelyn wasn't smiling. Mother's smile faded.

"Isn't that what you wanted?" An expression of puzzlement covered her features.

"Of course it is, Mama. I now know how he feels about me, but something isn't quite right. I just have a bad feeling."

"Why don't you ask him?"

"Guess I could, but I hate to overstep the boundaries."

The smile on her mother's face returned. "I don't think he'd consider you overstepping *any* boundaries, not with how he feels about you, Katelyn."

Still, Katelyn didn't wish to invade James's privacy. She didn't feel as though she had any right. It bothered her that James hadn't acted on his words and started a more conventional relationship between them.

"I just don't know," she confided to her mother. "He said something else last night, and I'm not sure what it means."

"What?"

"He told John Dorman that he was having other problems, right after he informed him that he loved me."

"That could mean anything," her mother said. "I think you're letting your imagination run away with you."

"Maybe I am." Katelyn folded the cheesecloth and laid it beside the pail holding the warm medicinal tea. She would serve the remedy to the newcomers shortly.

"Could be," her mother suggested, "that he's worried about the mercantile, among other things. The store rests on his shoulders now."

"Yes, I know." Katelyn thought for a moment, biting her lower lip. "But James is perfectly capable of accepting that responsibility. He's worked beside his father for the better part of two years now. He knows the mercantile inside and out. Why would it be giving him such fits?"

"Maybe there's more to it than we realize." Her mother ran a hand over the folded nightshirt, obviously enjoying the feel of the soft flannel.

Lifting the pail of fresh sassafras tea by its handle, Katelyn studied her mother. "I'm just not sure about this."

"It'll be okay," the woman reassured her. "Remember to leave it in God's hands. Pray about it. 'Lean not on your own understanding. . . .' "

She knew her mother was right. Difficult as it was, Katelyn had to give everything to the Lord, not just what she chose to hand over. *Okay, Father in heaven, You direct my paths in all ways. I hand everything to you. Everything.*

Katelyn's mother left to replace the soiled nightshirt with the fresh garment. Then she busied herself with the children, feeding them pudding and biscuits.

Katelyn hadn't moved. She was trying to be open to God's leading. Just then, she glanced toward Martha's cot. The woman was not there. Panic filled her. Where could she have gone? Her eyes traveled the room, searching for Martha. Suddenly they stopped. Katelyn could hardly believe what she was seeing.

Martha had struggled out of bed. She'd knelt beside her sister, Maggie, stroking her hair and talking to her in a voice filled with pure compassion. Katelyn stepped closer.

"I'm so sorry, Maggie," she heard Martha say. "I've not been the sister, no, the person I should have been all these years. Will you forgive me?"

A barely audible yes escaped Maggie's fever-chapped lips.

"We only have each other," Martha continued, "and I'm praying for you now, Mags, I'm praying real hard. I don't want to lose you. Do you understand?"

"Yes."

"When this is done, we'll have to pull together. It's only you and me, now, but we can make it. I know we can." Martha paused, tears falling from her tired eyes. "And there are going to be some changes in how we run Father's estate. There are some things I want to talk with you about as soon as you're better."

With that, Martha planted a gentle kiss on her sister's

forehead and stood unsteadily.

"If you need anything," Martha added, "you just let me know. I'm going to take care of you from now on. Don't you worry." Quietly she made her way back to her cot and promptly fell asleep.

Tears fell the rest of that morning as Katelyn walked through her morning routine. It occurred to her that labeling the sick "newcomers" had just received new meaning. Martha was a newcomer in Christ. Katelyn would use that word the rest of her life. And she would seek to bring people to the Lord through her unique gift of healing. At last she understood her purpose for living.

ॐ

James entered the mercantile. It was the first time he'd paid attention to the store since his father's passing. Before he'd only entered to grab cloth needed for makeshift beds, then left without a backward glance. The memories were too fresh then. Now he closed his eyes and took a deep breath, enjoying the rich aroma of leather and coffee.

He studied the glass containers holding licorice, taffy, and bubble gum that rested along the top of the counter. It was as if he was viewing the mercantile for the first time, realizing it was his to run. How he missed his father!

His eyes scanned boots, ox yokes, hackamores, kettles, and animal traps hanging from the rafters. Bonnets, mirrors, hair combs, and colorful ribbons decorated a shelf in the corner of the store. Thick rolls of canvas and linen lay askew on the floor where he had unrolled and sliced sections for use in making the cots.

Bolts of muslin, calico, and gingham rested on a shelf in the women's section with a sign that read "Ladies' Merchandise" posted on a wire torso standing at attention in the corner.

An assortment of canned goods, sacks of flour, and coffee beans rested in a heap on the floor in front of the counter, unloaded from the last shipment. These James had to shelve.

He stepped to the counter and viewed several pieces of

torn papers lying there. As he read them, he realized people had come in and gathered supplies in his absence. They left their own tabs of the items taken and the costs. It made him smile. Cimarron had endured the storm. He wasn't so certain he'd survive his own gale winds, though.

The thought caused the smile to dissolve like sugar in hot water. He bent to lift some of the canned goods and began stacking them on the shelf lining the wall behind the counter. Work. He must work, try to get his mind off Katelyn and the thing he must do today. He would propose to Martha. It was time.

Two hours passed. Before James stepped outside, he grabbed several red ribbons of licorice and tucked the candy in his pocket. He left the mercantile door unlocked in case others needed supplies. The drizzle turned to a downpour. His Stetson secure on his head, James walked to his paint and mounted the animal. He set off, heading in the direction of the Fontanna homestead.

His gut tightened as he rode, the rain pelting him in the face and running in a stream off the brim of his hat. He didn't care. He wanted to fulfill the promise he'd made to his father—had to keep it. Then he'd move on and do the best he could with the life handed him.

It occurred to James that God hadn't answered this prayer, either. Maybe the Lord *was* angry at him for his past behavior. Yet he'd learned he wasn't being punished, and he wanted to accept what Katelyn had told Martha when she'd voiced similar concerns. It was too confusing. He didn't know what to believe. What did he have to do to get prayers answered? Was he to spend his entire life in a cycle of unhappiness? Justly deserved though that unhappiness might be, he had changed. Didn't that count for something? Or must he suffer for his mistakes for eternity? A shiver ran through him.

Before long, James could clearly see the Fontanna soddie on the horizon. It was nearing the noon hour, and dark gray clouds hovered above. A chill breeze cooled the air. As he dismounted, James noticed the men who usually stayed to help with building projects and various repairs were nowhere in sight. There jobs had been finished. They were no longer needed at the soddie and had left to get their own lives back in order.

Securing his paint out front, James moved up onto the porch, opened the door, and stepped inside. The sight of Katelyn feeding lunch to one of the patients warmed him. Quickly he squelched the feeling, knowing he should not be encouraging himself to yearn.

Katelyn glanced toward the door, thankful that James had returned. She watched as he removed his hat, stepped to the hearth, and set the Stetson next to the fire where it could dry. He nodded in her direction, and Katelyn returned the nod with a wave and a slight smile.

Warmth filled her chest and rose into her cheeks when she saw him walk over to the playing children, tug something from his pocket, and kneel down before them, grinning. He handed them the goodies. Carrie clapped her hands in glee, and Toby wasted no time in chewing on the sweet, nodding a silent *thank you*.

Dropping her gaze back to her task, Katelyn fed the final spoonful of molasses-sweetened mush to her newcomer. She continued to study James from the corner of her eye. His smile faded when he stood. He strode to Maggie's cot and talked to her in calming tones. James touched her arm gently now and then as he spoke his assurance for her well-being.

How special you are, James, Katelyn told herself. Then her mother approached.

"Katelyn, we have to do something about Mrs. Chardoneau."

"I agree," Katelyn said, "but how?"

"We've got to get that babe away, give him a proper Christian burial, and start on her treatments. I fear it'll be too late if we wait much longer." The older woman clenched her hands, showing white knuckles of distress.

Glancing toward the Cheyenne widow, Katelyn wondered

how Mrs. Chardoneau might react when they took the dead infant from her arms. "I think she holds onto him as her last link," she said. Then Katelyn stood, clutching the tin plate and spoon in both hands. "She's among strangers here, Mama. We'll have to be *very* gentle."

Her glance shifted to James as he stepped away from Maggie's cot and made his way to Martha's bed. She turned her head to look at her mother again, agonizing over the worry she saw in the woman's green eyes. Looking down at the freshly swept puncheon floor, Katelyn pulled her bottom lip in between her teeth. She bit down too hard. A tiny drop of blood rose on her otherwise smooth mouth, but she paid it no attention.

She spoke softly. "We'll need James to stand by, in case she puts up a fight."

Her mother nodded in agreement.

Again, Katelyn gazed in James's direction. He sat on the edge of Martha's cot, his back to them, gently nudging the woman awake.

Looking at her mother, Katelyn said, "I'll go talk with James and see if he'll help us."

Her mother ran her hands nervously up and down both arms, as though struggling to warm herself. "I'll get the children settled on the porch and make sure they're out of harm's way."

At this, Katelyn's mother stepped to where Toby and Carrie played contentedly while thunder reverberated outside. She spoke to them in hushed tones.

Katelyn smiled despite herself when she watched the children's eyes open wide with a spirit of adventure. She didn't know what her mother had told them, but it had obviously worked.

Next, her mother gripped two army blankets and wrapped the two children securely. They still clutched the licorice James had given them. Then she led them outside onto the covered porch, clear of the rain. She stayed out with them for a few moments, then returned, closing the door gently.

While her mother busied herself with other tasks, Katelyn stepped to the table, setting the plate and spoon down on its rough pine top. She eyed three fresh loaves of bread, some Johnny cakes, and a batch of sorghum cookies left by Beth the evening before.

Focusing on what she must do, Katelyn made her way to James. Approaching from behind, she moved close enough to catch his attention when she spoke. He was still talking to Martha, who lay sleepy eyed on her cot.

Not wanting to interrupt, Katelyn waited patiently for a pause in their conversation. She cleared her throat to alert him of her presence, but he seemed not to notice.

"I'm glad you're feeling better, Martha," James said. "I knew you'd pull through."

"Only by the grace of God, James," Martha offered. "Now, I'm praying for my little sister."

James nodded, stiffened, seemed to brace himself. "There's something I need to ask you, Martha. Been meaning to for some time now, but never got around to it."

Fidgeting, Katelyn wanted to step away. She glanced in the direction of the Cheyenne woman, where she sat clutching her baby in the corner opposite them. But when Katelyn saw James go down on one knee, she froze, her gaze fixed in amazement.

"Martha," James began, gripping one of her hands in both of his. "Will. . .will you marry me?"

Katelyn's mouth went dry. Her heart pounded so hard and fast she could hear it beating in her ears like a freight train hammering down a nearby stretch of track.

James turned when he heard the gasp. *Katelyn! Why are you looking at me like that?* A cry escaped his throat. He'd been wrong about Katelyn! He could see it in her eyes. When tears threatened to brim over and fall down her cheeks, he knew without doubt. She felt the same about him as he did toward her. And now he had broken her heart.

Rising, James struggled with what he should do next. He had just asked one woman to marry him while his true love stood by and watched. Both Katelyn and Martha seemed to wait for his next move. The passing moments hovered like sand in an hour glass, falling at an agonizingly slow rate.

"Katelyn," he mouthed, the word barely audible as it passed through his lips.

"James?" Martha asked.

He passed his gaze from Katelyn to Martha, then back again to the woman he loved. He watched Katelyn grip her long chestnut-colored locks in one hand and fan her back with its length.

Her face suddenly void of expression, she stepped up to him. The only remaining signs of her shock were unspent tears pooling in her eyes like rushing water that had been dammed and redirected.

"James," she began, "we'll be needing your help. If you will."

Still gripping Martha's hand, James nodded. "Of course," he said, "anything."

If only he could be swallowed up by the cracks in the plank wood floor. His heart lodged in his throat. He knew he must fulfill the promise he'd made his father. But, how? The image of Katelyn standing there burned into him like a raging fire that could not be controlled. It would have to burn itself out, and James knew that would take a lifetime.

His struggle between the promise he'd made to his father and his love for Katelyn caused a cold sweat to break out on his forehead and around the base of his neck.

Katelyn spoke again, her voice tremulous. "We need to take the baby from Mrs. Chardoneau, and we might need your help."

James managed a nod. Martha called his name again, a slight pleading quality in her tone. He knew he couldn't continue to ignore her. Giving Martha's slim hand a brief squeeze of reassurance, he asked Katelyn, "Can you give me a few minutes?"

She nodded. He watched her drop her gaze, turn, and walk slowly toward the slat-backed rocker, where she sat heavily, as though she could no longer hold her weight.

"James?" Martha called again.

He turned to face her square, torment reflected in his brown gaze. He repeated his question. "Will you marry me, Martha?"

The smile stretching her lips made his heart grow cold. He waited with apprehension. How could he not have known about Katelyn? How? *Maybe I made myself believe it,* he thought. *Maybe it's not even true.*

"James," Martha said. "I accept your proposal."

fifteen

"Under one condition," Martha added, the smile playing tenderly on her lips.

Of course, James thought, *always conditions with Martha.* "What?" he asked dryly. A promise was a promise, and he would do whatever Martha asked of him to fulfill it.

Martha withdrew her hands from his grasp and rested them across the front of the patchwork quilt covering her. "Under the condition that you can tell me you *truly* love me."

James balked, his eyes widening in surprise. "What?"

"Do you truly love me, James? As you should love your wife? Can you tell me that, without doubt? I want only the truth."

Resting his weight on his other foot, James studied Martha. "I–I don't understand."

Lifting herself up on one elbow, Martha rested her head in the palm of her right hand, her fingertips touching the crown of her head. She looked up at James with a clear blue gaze.

He knew she was perfectly lucid, the fever no longer claiming hold of her body. The only signs of sickness were the slowly healing lesions covering her face. Scar tissue created purplish-pink spots, dipping into otherwise smooth skin.

"Please answer the question," Martha said in a soft, almost whispery voice.

James threw his glance in Katelyn's direction, then back to Martha again. "I'm simply asking for your hand in marriage," he stated. He paused, studied her. "Martha, I've already received the blessing from your folks," he went on. "Talked with your father some time ago."

He saw Martha's eyes gloss over with tears. She cleared her throat.

"I'm sorry, Martha," he said, "I didn't mean to upset you." He thought the tears in Martha's eyes unusual. Generally, if she cried at all, it was for herself. A sense of bafflement caused his brows to furrow, giving his stare a tense quality.

She kept to the subject, sniffing back tears. "Do you love me, James?"

"No, I don't. Not the way a wife might expect," James finally answered, "but I do care about you, Martha, and. . .and I'm sure I'll grow to love you like that as time passes."

"I can't accept your proposal then, James." She hesitated only briefly, brushed his hand with her fingers, then retreated from the touch. "I'm sorry."

At first James said nothing. When he finally spoke, he wasn't sure if the words would make it past the lump lodged in his throat. "I don't understand."

He saw Martha look in Katelyn's direction, where she waited, reading the Bible.

"It's Katelyn McKnight you need to be proposing to."

James reached up and rubbed his left temple, but quickly let his hand back down to hang at his side. That felt uncomfortable, so he slipped his left thumb into a loop holding his belt snug to his jeans.

"James," Martha continued, "there was a time when I wanted this more than anything in the world. But there's a change occurring in me. . .for the better."

"Guess I still don't understand, Martha," James told her. "If this is what you wanted—"

"Oh, believe me," Martha inserted, "I absolutely wanted to marry you before. . .before I lost my loved ones and then got sick myself."

"Go on." Curiosity claimed James in a grip so tight, it constricted his breathing. A sensation of hope began to edge out the despair that earlier had flooded his heart.

Drawing a deep breath, Martha spoke. "I felt so empty, James, so very empty. That's why I began drinking. Seemed my father's money couldn't fill the void in my spirit, no matter how many silk evening gowns or velvet hats or expensive jewels were laid at my feet."

James's features relaxed. His shoulders dropped as though strings of tension had been cut. He continued to listen, almost disbelievingly.

"I want my life to mean something, James," she continued. "Jesus fills that void now." She paused. "I want to leave something tangible behind when I go to be with the Lord, not just empty hat boxes." She pointed a finger at Katelyn. "She's a good example of what Christianity is all about. And I'm working in that direction."

Martha rested her head back on the feather pillow and studied James. "And it's Katelyn McKnight you need to be making this request of. I've seen it in your eyes." She paused. "And, I've seen it in her eyes, too, James."

"I do love Katelyn." James surprised himself with the statement.

"Then go to her," Martha advised. "Ask her to be your wife."

It suddenly occurred to James that God *had* answered his prayer, had been working on it all along. He just hadn't been able to see it. He vowed right then never to doubt the Lord again. Martha wasn't the only one who had been changed through this experience.

Martha interrupted his thoughts. "James, I want to apologize for the way I've been in the past."

James lifted a hand in the air to halt her words. "Martha, there's no need—"

"I have to say this," she insisted.

Acknowledging her need with a nod, he found himself drawn to this changed woman. She seemed so different. Even her voice had a softer lilt to it. Her features appeared less constricted, more beautiful, despite the pock marks.

"I've been very selfish to everyone and to my Lord and Savior. I want to start changing things now. I've learned so much James." Martha cried softly.

Wrapping his fingers around her trembling chin, James gave it a gentle squeeze. "I've learned a lot, too, Martha. And you're not the only one who's made mistakes. We all have. I've made plenty myself, more than I'd care to admit."

"I–I want to do what's right now," she continued, smiling through her tears. "And. . .and I want to marry a man who will love me, not simply tolerate me."

"The man you marry, Martha, will be a very blessed individual."

"Thank you." Martha dabbed at her tears and set her chin. "I also want to turn my home, the home of the late Gabe Appleburg, into a hospital for Cimarron."

"You don't need to do that, Martha!"

"You don't understand, James. I can't live there any longer. I've lost most of my family. We lived there together with lots of happy memories." She watched Katelyn again.

"That woman. . ." She hesitated. "The woman you love has a very special gift. If she can supply the nursing part of the gift, then I want to supply what's needed for her to work. Between both of us, we can make a difference." She turned her attention back to James.

"I do want us to remain friends, James, if that's okay with you."

His answer was a soft kiss to her forehead.

"Now, go," Martha told him. "You have some things to work out." The smile on her full mouth kissed her eyes, causing them to sparkle. "I'll be praying for you."

James drew a deep breath, trying to comprehend his new situation. Everything had changed. His life seemed to be gaining direction. "I'll be needing your prayers," he said with renewed conviction in the power of prayer.

He turned away from Martha on the cot. As he gazed upon Katelyn, a myriad of thoughts crashed into his mind, making him feel edgy again. *No. Use your faith,* he warned himself. *You've been shown. Don't start doubting now!*

Katelyn noticed movement and set the Bible down in her lap. James made quick strides to reach her.

"Katy, I need to speak with you."

Standing, Katelyn rested the volume on the rocker's seat. She rubbed her hands together. "We'll have to talk later, James. We really need to take care of Mrs. Chardoneau first."

James raked long fingers through his wavy mass of black hair, giving it a windswept appearance. "All right," he said. "What do you need me to do?"

Katelyn's mother approached. "Are we ready?"

"Yes," Katelyn answered, feeling a sense of dread come over her. This feeling was not as powerful as the emotions that had hit her when she'd heard James proposing to Martha, but they were strong enough.

At the livery stable, she'd heard James say her name. Why, then, had he just proposed to another woman? Did this have to do with the other problems of which he spoke? None of it made sense.

Numbness flooded her being. It was not meant to be. *Your will be done, Father.* She felt as though James had taken a knife and sliced a ravine through her heart. Katelyn fought back tears. Then she gave herself a mental shake. There was work to be done, and she had to do it.

"Let me go to her, first," Katelyn said to the two people awaiting her instructions. "She seems to trust me." She studied the floor, not able to look directly into James's eyes as she addressed him.

"James," she explained, "we'll need you to stand by just in case things get out of hand."

"No problem."

Katelyn's mother clenched a section of her percale skirt in her right fist. "Let's hope things *won't* get out of hand."

Katelyn turned and began her approach. Sorrow flooded her eyes at the sight. Mrs. Chardoneau could barely balance herself on the balls of her feet as she sat in the corner. She gripped the infant tightly, her eyes wild with fever and fear. Her hair was no longer woven in braids, but had come loose over the days since her arrival. The sprigs of sage ornamenting her braids had fallen out. Missing, also, was the copper bracelet previously worn on her upper right arm.

Katelyn noticed that her mother hung back, watching, waiting. James kept his own distance, but stood a little closer.

Mrs. Chardoneau never looked up, even as Katelyn knelt in front of the woman. Katelyn studied her eyes. They looked as though she was in another world, not with them. Over and over, she uttered incoherent words and phrases and made hand gestures as though she conversed with imaginary people. Though the woman lived, breathed, Katelyn saw no life in those brown eyes. And her trembling told Katelyn it was only with great effort that she didn't faint to the ground.

Slowly, Katelyn stretched her hands out toward Mrs. Chardoneau, palms upward. The frightened woman clutched her infant tighter. She would have squeezed the life out of the baby by now, had the child not passed on already.

Then Katelyn spoke, knowing her words meant nothing to the sick woman but hoping the tone in them might soothe her.

"Give me the child," she said. "Let me take care of him for you." As the words were spoken, Katelyn reached fingers out to touch the soft deerskin covering the baby.

A wild cry rent the air as the woman rose to her feet and took a stance that told Katelyn to back away.

Carefully Katelyn rose to her feet as well, holding her ground. Her heart raced in her chest. She worked hard to control her body and keep from making any abrupt movements. "It's okay," Katelyn soothed, speaking softly.

Somebody cried out. Maggie. She'd obviously been awakened by the woman's screams. Katelyn threw her glance toward where the young girl wrestled against herself on the cot across the room. She was relieved to see Martha get out of bed and go to her sister.

All the other newcomers were awake and seemed to understand what was happening, for they remained quiet and still.

A red tinge showed through the woman's dark brown skin. Welts dotted her features. Katelyn knew these would open soon and begin oozing with infection. Mrs. Chardoneau hadn't eaten since her arrival, and Katelyn wondered when the last time was that she'd taken any nourishment or fluid. The disease would surely claim her, and fast, if they didn't take control of the situation.

The Indian woman was about Katelyn's height and weight. Katelyn firmly believed she could handle a struggle should the woman choose to fight. Yet the wild fear consuming Mrs. Chardoneau warned Katelyn she might be wrong.

She stole a glance at James for security's sake, then with a darting motion, she yanked the baby from the Cheyenne woman's grasp. Intense pain filled Katelyn's head. Then everything went black.

sixteen

Katelyn woke to a cold sensation on her forehead, running down along her throat and shoulders. She studied the face hovering above through blurred vision. Slowly, she regained her focus.

"Oh, honey," her mother murmured. "Are you okay?"

"W–what happened?" Katelyn struggled to sit up.

"No, no," her mother warned. "Stay here for a while longer."

"Can't." With great effort, Katelyn pulled her feet under her and stood, unsteadily at first. "What happened?" she repeated.

Her mother pointed to the corner of the room. Katelyn followed the finger with her gaze. James had pinned the Indian woman to the ground and was speaking to her calmly but firmly. "I'm not going to hurt you," he said, repeating the phrase several times. "Just be still."

"When you grabbed the babe," Katelyn's mother explained, "she clasped her hands together and swung at your head with a force I've never seen come from a woman in my life!"

Katelyn detected a hint of anger in her mother's voice and realized she must calm her down. "Mama, I'm okay," she reminded the woman. "Mrs. Chardoneau is frightened."

When the intensity on her mother's face failed to relax, Katelyn continued. "How would you feel if somebody ripped me from your arms? Or little Carrie?"

Her mother sighed with reluctant understanding. "Yes," she responded. "I would have fought, too." She reached up and ran a willowy finger over the knot forming on Katelyn's cheek bone. "Mothers can be very protective of their children. I know I am."

Wincing, Katelyn withdrew from the touch. The injured area

hurt as if the skin had been burned. "I'm fine, Mama." She glanced in James's direction. "We need to get Mrs. Chardoneau to a cot."

Both Katelyn and Abigail jumped when Martha approached from behind.

"She can have my cot," Martha offered. "I'm feeling strong enough to start helping out around here."

Studying her, Katelyn drew her bottom lip in between her teeth, careful not to bite down too hard. How different she was from the old Martha. It reminded Katelyn of Paul in the Bible and the change that occurred in him. Of course, she acknowledged to herself, James had witnessed this *new* Martha and couldn't help falling in love with her. The woman was still beautiful, despite the pock marks covering her face. And she was wealthy in her own right. Add that to the change in her nature, and the draw might be overwhelming.

But much as Katelyn understood and wished the couple well, she couldn't deny her own pain. It sliced through her heart with the ferocity of an attacking grizzly. It felt odd to have such mixed feelings wrestling inside of her. She would act toward James and Martha with the Christian love and respect they deserved and pray that in time God would heal her wounded heart.

"She can have my cot," Martha repeated.

Katelyn jumped, realizing that her thoughts had drawn her completely away from the conversation. "That's very kind of you, Martha," she said. "But are you sure you're strong enough?"

Martha nodded. "I've noticed my strength returning with each day that passes. I really want to help now, not just lie around doing nothing. I want to give back. I've already received so much. I want to give back," she repeated.

Dumbfounded, Katelyn studied Martha's clear blue gaze. "Thank you so much, Martha. That's good. Very good."

Quietly Katelyn stepped to where James restrained Mrs. Chardoneau. The woman wasn't uttering a sound. No tears fell. Fear consumed her wide brown eyes, sending a shiver racing up Katelyn's spine.

"Can you manage to get her onto Martha's cot?" she asked James.

Sweat formed like tiny blisters along James's upper lip and forehead. "I'll give it a try."

With that, he slipped one arm beneath the Indian woman's shoulders and the other beneath her knees. This sent Mrs. Chardoneau into a new panic. James spoke soothing words as he carried the young woman, kicking and screaming, to Martha's cot.

As soon as he laid her down, she ceased struggling. Katelyn noted her breathing had turned to mere gasps. Her eyes fought to roll back beneath her lids.

The fight she had just put up, Katelyn surmised, would only add to the severity of her illness. But Katelyn was determined not to lose hope. So far, they had saved more people than they'd lost, which was virtually unheard of with an epidemic of these proportions. God's love and mercy combined with their efforts and prayers yielded the results they witnessed. Katelyn believed this with all her heart.

Mrs. Chardoneau was simply the latest challenge. And Katelyn knew it would not be an easy thing to bring the woman back to health. The illness had a stronger hold on the woman than it had had on many of the other patients. The others came into Katelyn's care at the onset of the disease.

The trader and his wife may have brought the smallpox to Cimarron. They were obviously the first to get sick. Of course, the Indian woman would not know how to help her husband, how to ask for help. She only did so when it was too late, when she knew her husband was nearing death, when desperation forced her to go against her fears. Katelyn's thoughts were interrupted by Martha's voice.

"Poor thing," she observed. "She's so frightened." Martha stepped over to the woman, looking down on her with eyes filled with compassion.

James moved away from the cot, cautiously at first, as though anticipating another tussle. When none came, Katelyn could see his shoulders relax. He nursed his left wrist, then glanced Katelyn's way. Slowly he walked to where she stood beside her mother.

"You okay?" he asked.

"Yes. I'm fine, thank you." Katelyn looked over in Mrs. Chardoneau's direction. It pleased her to see Martha cooling the woman's fever with cool, wet cloths. Although Martha tried to persuade her to drink, however, Mrs. Chardoneau refused.

James's voice broke into her thoughts. "Katy, are you sure you're all right?" He started to rest a comforting hand on her shoulder, but Katelyn pulled back.

The pain wasn't in the injury from Mrs. Chardoneau's attack, she wanted to tell James. Rather, the injury was in her heart. No physical pain could compare. Tears threatened to free themselves from the prison of her lashes. How would she ever get past this torment? *Lord, help me.*

To her dismay, James gripped her by the right shoulder. "You don't look all right to me," he said, concern filling his voice. "Come sit down." With that, he led her to the pine bench beside the table. He dipped the ladle into a bucket of water and handed it to Katelyn. "Drink some of this. It'll help you feel better."

Katelyn drank what she could. It did seem to soothe the pain throbbing in her temples.

"I'll get you some tea," her mother offered, making her way past cots to the hearth. She returned, handing a tumbler to Katelyn. "This might help." She seemed to study her daughter. "We might need to apply cold compresses to that injury."

Reaching up, Katelyn feathered slender fingers over the raised area. "No, really, I'm fine." She couldn't look directly at James. "It's already going down."

"If you're sure. . ."

"Yes, Mama, I'm sure." Katelyn caught James studying

her, as one might gauge a target prior to shooting. His stare made her fidget. She stood, feeling her balance return.

"Need to get back to work," she announced abruptly, leaving James and her mother to deal with their confusion and concern.

"I hope she's all right," James said, watching Abigail take the seat Katelyn had just occupied.

The older woman wiped her hands on the apron secured around her middle. "I'm not sure what's wrong with my daughter," she said. "She seems preoccupied." She peered into James's eyes. "I'm worried about her. Wish I knew what the problem might be."

Did James detect a hint of suspicion in Abigail's tone? He cleared his throat. It was only natural that the mother of the woman he loved would try to discover her child's dilemma, try to ease her troubles.

"Can you step out back?" James asked. "I'll explain things the best I can."

Relief covered his face when he saw a smile form on Abigail's lips. She was an understanding woman, and besides, he thought, he needed to talk with somebody! Since Martha had rejected his proposal, he'd felt that his world was in total chaos. He'd set his mind to keeping the promise he'd made to his dying father, no matter how difficult that might prove to be. Now he was freed from that obligation and had no idea what to do. Maybe Abigail could offer some direction.

ﾑ

Katelyn never saw her mother and James leave. Her back was to them as she stoked the fire in the hearth, adding buffalo chips to raise the heat. The rain had eased to a mere drizzle, though the sky continued its angry torrent of thunder and lightning.

Katelyn wandered onto the porch and led the children back inside. They ate biscuits and played with a young boy who had survived his smallpox ordeal and was feeling well enough to grow fidgety at being confined to bed.

Martha visited with Maggie, providing the same loving care

as she had shared with Mrs. Chardoneau. Katelyn glanced toward the Indian woman where she lay still as a stone on the cot. The young mother stared at the ceiling as though in deep thought. Katelyn wondered what she might be thinking. *You're probably missing your husband and son.* Her heart grew heavy with compassion. It made her remember her own losses. Quickly she cleared her throat, as though the effort might dash the memories away. No. Only occupying herself would help.

She mouthed a quick prayer and set to her tasks. She would need to cook a batch of onions and mix it with honey to ease a deep cough one of the newcomers had developed. It was then that Katelyn realized her mother was gone. She searched the interior of the soddie and discovered James missing as well. Katelyn left the onions to brown in the skillet resting directly over the coals. Curiosity propelled her to the front porch.

Familiar, yet barely discernible voices came from the back of the home. Katelyn made her way around to the back end of one of the side walls. Her hands touched thickly matted grass roots knitted into the mud barricade. *What are they talking about?* she wondered.

It occurred to Katelyn she was eavesdropping yet again. Curious or not, she forced herself to turn and trudge back to the porch, making her way to the door. Entering the soddie, Katelyn's muscles tightened.

Mrs. Chardoneau had escaped.

❧

"I love your daughter," James explained. "Yet I had no choice but to propose to Martha."

Confusion settled in Abigail's green eyes. "I don't quite understand," she told him. "You love Katelyn, yet you proposed to Martha?"

"Yes, ma'am." James cleared his throat. "Let me explain." He started at the beginning.

When he'd completed the story, Abigail put her hand on his shoulder. "You've had a hard time of it," she said. "I had no idea the pressure you were under. But it does explain things,

things that were beginning to confuse me, to be truthful."

"I'm sorry about the confusion," James told her. "I really had no idea my problems would cause problems for anybody else, except Katelyn, of course."

"She loves you, James. You know that, don't you?"

"I know that now. I didn't know it at the time, though. Thought it was a one-sided matter."

"No, not at all." Abigail hesitated. "What will you do now?"

James pondered the question. Finally he said, "I know I may be out of order, here, b. . .but I'd like to ask for your daughter's hand in marriage."

"Have you asked her yet?"

"No, ma'am," he answered. "But I intend to, if we can have your blessing." Before Abigail could respond, James added, "I don't even know if she'll accept me now. She's been hurt so much, I can't even imagine."

A tiny laugh filled the ensuing silence. "That daughter of mine has a good head on her shoulders," Abigail stated. "If you explain things, I'm sure she'll understand. Just as I understand."

Does this mean I have your blessing? James couldn't bring himself to ask the question again but prayed it was so. Abigail's next words caused all doubt on the issue to end.

"Go to her," Abigail told him. "You have my blessing."

Without another word, the two headed back to the soddie, but when they entered, Martha greeted them, tears of worry filling her eyes. The burning scent of onions filled the air.

"She's gone," Martha nearly choked. "Mrs. Chardoneau took off, and Katelyn's gone after her! It's all my fault."

Abigail put her arms around Martha, trying to comfort her. But a different concern filled James. If Katelyn didn't catch up to the Cheyenne woman, they stood to shoulder the responsibility of infecting an entire Indian nation.

Even if Katelyn *did* manage to track Mrs. Chardoneau down, could she handle the frightened woman? Stop her? Katelyn's life was in danger.

"I'm going after them," James declared without another thought. "Get that pan of onions off the fire before the place burns down."

Abigail moved to the task but said nothing. Then she retrieved a parfleche, which she filled with biscuits and corn pones. She handed it to James. "Please bring my daughter home," she said quietly.

James left, forgetting his Stetson still drying near the fireplace. Both mules were missing. When he mounted his paint, thunder broke the air. The horse bolted. Yanking hard on the reins, he turned the beast in a circle until it settled. Then James kicked the horse hard in the sides and took off at a dead run.

The tracks left were easy to follow. Mule hooves had left deep gashes in the prairie mud, which were now filling with water like tiny pools. Rain wet his face, pouring off his chin like a deluge of unrestrained tears.

James knew his horse was faster than the mules and believed he would catch up to them shortly. Still, as he studied the landscape, he saw the women were nowhere in sight. The tracks extended east, southeast. James launched into ravines, rounded bends, and climbed bluffs. He struggled to sidestep the abundant yucca, prickly pear cactus, and nodding thistle that dotted the landscape. Fear filled his heart. He had been so close to setting things straight, claiming Katelyn's heart once and for all. Now he faced the risk of losing her, just when—

Struggling to control his emotions, James pressed onward. When his vision caught a bluff ahead, he forced himself to believe he would discover them on the other side. That wasn't the case.

What he'd thought would be a quick search stretched into hours. James tugged on the reins to slow his horse to a lope, even walked it some, knowing the animal's stamina might weaken. Mules, though they moved at a slower pace, harbored more stamina than a horse, and he didn't want their endurance to gain them victory over his horse.

Finally James stopped so his paint could nibble bunch grass and squelch its thirst from a buffalo wallow filled with rainwater. He stayed atop his steed, studying the land. Additional bluffs and draws cut into the edge of the vista, obscuring his view. The women could be anywhere.

"Please, Lord, let her be okay," James said out loud. "You're the only One I can truly depend on, and I'm trusting You with all my heart."

James shoved onward. Another hour passed until he finally arrived at the point where McClellan Creek ran into the North Fork of the Red River. He knew the area as well as any scout. There were caves nearby.

Cliffs rose on both sides as James rode along the bank of the river. The rain stopped abruptly, and a strange peace settled over the rough country. Peering upward, he glimpsed an eagle, wings spread wide, soaring. James took a deep breath and continued his search.

When he topped a draw heading north, he heard the noises. They sounded like the cries a wounded animal might make, yet they were strangely human. The sounds echoed all around him, and he had a little difficulty determining from which direction they came.

He followed the wails to the mouth of a cave, lined in gypsum and moss. To his relief, he spotted the mules. One roamed freely; the other had been tethered to a nearby thicket. Then the cries ended abruptly.

Lines of worry creased his forehead. His heart raced. Could they have come from Katelyn? Had some wild animal ravaged her?

"Katy!" he yelled. "Katy!"

Dismounting, James let his horse loose. He dashed to the cave opening. When he stooped inside, he spotted them. Holding Mrs. Chardoneau in her arms, Katelyn sat, tears streaming down her cheeks. Her breath came in spasms as though she'd been running a footrace.

His features softened, and he stepped to Katelyn, kneeling down before her where she rested against the damp cave wall. A stream of water coursed past them, leaving their sight as it entered a tunnel at the back of the cave.

"She's gone," Katelyn informed him, chin trembling.

James nodded. He studied her through eyes filled with compassion and empathy. She had taken about as much as any one person could.

"We'll take her back," James said, gripping Katelyn by the arm and pulling her to her feet. He led her from the dampness of the cave, outside to where the sun struggled to peek through storm clouds.

She dried her eyes and drew a deep breath. "What are you doing here?"

"Came after you."

Katelyn said nothing. James knew what he must do, and he would do it right this moment before anything else could cause yet another interruption.

"Now," he told her, "we need to talk."

"James, this is not the time nor the place."

He chuckled. "I've learned the hard way that there is no right time or place." He cleared his throat, allowing the smile to linger on his lips. "There will be no more waiting. And you need to listen to me."

"Listen?"

"That's what I said, Katy. You need to *listen* to me."

"Go ahead, then, if you must." She sniffed and dabbed at more tears, seeming to struggle with her emotions.

"First," he began, "I am so sorry you have suffered through this ordeal."

"We all have suffered, James. All of us."

"Yes, I know that, but I mean I'm sorry you suffered for a different reason."

She swallowed hard. "Guess I don't understand."

"Let me explain, then. Explain everything."

James told his story from the beginning, ending with his

proposal to Martha. Then he explained why Martha had refused him.

For a long moment, Katelyn didn't move, didn't speak. She wrapped her arms around herself as though needing a hug. A tiny tear coursed down her cheek. James watched her lift her beautiful eyes heavenward. Following her gaze, he glanced in the same direction.

A double rainbow loomed overhead, like some colorful miracle in the sky. The eagle he had seen before soared within the arch of the rainbow.

"The promise," Katelyn whispered. "The storm of sickness in Cimarron is over."

But James claimed the rainbow as a sign of his own, a sign of the love that would blossom between the two of them, each brilliant color representing a future chapter of their lives.

The pinks and lavenders, to him, represented the passion they would know. The blue represented the labors they would perform together. And the oranges and yellows ignited the commitment between them that no one could break once bound under God.

Again, he rested his gaze on the woman he loved. There was one more thing he must do. Gripping her small hand in his large one, he dropped to one knee before her.

When she drew her bottom lip in between her teeth, he smiled. She only did that when she was nervous. He loved everything about her, even her mannerisms.

"Katy," he began, "I love you. You know that, don't you?"

She nodded. A tiny hiccup rose in her chest. "I love you, too, James," she whispered.

"Then I want to ask you something."

Again, Katelyn nodded, keeping her gaze on James.

"Will you marry me? Will you be my wife?"

Disbelief settled in her tear-filled green eyes. A long moment of silence followed. James felt his heart race, but he remained on one knee before her, trying not to tremble.

When she finally spoke, he couldn't make out her words. "What?" he asked.

"Yes," she repeated, a smile touching her lips, filling her eyes with light.

With that he rose to his feet and circled his arms around her waist. He drew her to him in an embrace that chased all the agony of the past weeks away. Then gently he brushed her nose with his own, breathing in her scent. He caressed her neck and chin with his lips until he found the spot he was seeking.

Their lips met and held in a unifying force that filled him with a delight he'd never before experienced. How sweet Katelyn McKnight was. With great effort, he pulled back and studied her eyes. A calm had settled in their depths, a calm he had never witnessed before.

"Are you hungry?" he asked.

"Not really," Katelyn answered, "but I probably should eat something. Did you bring food?"

Walking to his animal and relieved it hadn't wandered off, James managed to loop the reins around the same thicket to which one of the mules was secured. The other mule was nowhere to be seen.

Retrieving his parfleche, he crossed back over to Katelyn's side and dipped a hand into the hide sack. He handed her a corn pone, which she readily took. James managed to down a couple himself. A grin covered his face when he looked at Katelyn.

Gently he brushed away a few yellow crumbs from her mouth. "There," he said.

A red tinge rose in Katelyn's cheeks.

"The blushing bride," he joked. She laughed, the color in her cheeks subsiding.

"Let's get back," he said. "Your mother's worried."

They both walked back into the cave.

seventeen

Katelyn and James rode home together on the paint, while the mule carried the body of the Indian woman. They never could find the other mule. They made it back by late evening. After dropping Katelyn off, James made his way into Cimarron to assist in the burial of Mrs. Chardoneau. They placed her beside her husband and infant son.

After the ceremony, James returned to the mercantile to bathe. It had been too long. Tomorrow, he decided, he'd open the doors of Connor Mercantile as a business again. His desire was to provide for his wife-to-be in the best way he could. James was going to live life fully, properly. He believed in a future once more. He would heed his late father's advice: *Teach the family in the ways of the Lord.*

He dressed in fresh clothes, a brown cotton shirt and jeans. After a shave, James entered the mercantile and began the arduous task of cleaning up the place. Things were in complete disarray from customers wandering in and out. He'd prepare invoices and inventory his goods. Soon he'd send out an order to replenish the supplies that had dwindled. But James was confident. He had no doubt that the business would regain momentum.

As he swept the puncheon floor and shook out rugs, James pondered the turns his life had taken. He knew God worked all things together for good for those who loved Him. Cimarron was a good example of that.

When thoughts of Katelyn entered his mind, a smile broke out on his lips, stretching them taut. He couldn't see the glow in his eyes as he worked into the night.

ও

Katelyn's mother hugged her, followed by a relieved Martha.

161

"Are you all right?" they both asked.

Giggling, Katelyn responded, "More than all right."

Though Martha wore a baffled expression, the look on Mother's face held perfect understanding. Katelyn explained everything. She'd followed Mrs. Chardoneau to the caves located near the North Fork of the Red River. Mrs. Chardoneau had obviously fallen from the mule as the sickness sought to claim her life. Katelyn found her just inside the cave, where she crawled, barely breathing. Prior to her passing, she sent up heartrending cries.

"I believe that's how James was able to locate me. I wasn't sure I could even find my way back," Katelyn explained. "I just followed her without paying any attention to where I was going."

"Our Lord was watching out for you," Katelyn's mother stated, her voice tremulous.

"Yes," Martha agreed. "He's watching out for us all." She stepped closer to Katelyn. "There's something I want to do," she added. "Something I feel the Lord would have me do."

"What's that?" Katelyn questioned.

Running a finger in and out of a wayward ringlet, Martha managed a slight smile. "We've. . .the people of Cimarron have been through so much." She paused. "I'd like to throw another barn dance in celebration of new beginnings for our town and its people."

Neither Katelyn nor her mother said a word.

Martha continued. "I'd like the celebration to serve as a housewarming of sorts for the new hospital."

Wrinkling her brow in puzzlement, Katelyn asked, "What new hospital?"

"I told James all about it," Martha said. "My home is to be the new hospital and. . .and I want you to head it, Katelyn. And you too, Abigail," she hurriedly added.

The right words with which to respond eluded Katelyn. Her mother answered for them both. "Martha, that's wonderful! You don't know how badly Cimarron needs something like this!"

"Oh, yes, I do," Martha contended. "All too well, actually."

"B. . .but where will you live, Martha?" Katelyn asked.

"With us, of course!" her mother said. "And Maggie, too. Even Toby," she added. With a smile, she said, "Our home will be filled with people and laughter once again. We'll all be a family. Lord knows I need the diversion."

"Thank you," Martha offered. Then she looked at Katelyn. "See, it's all taken care of. And Cimarron will have a hospital."

"Yes," Katelyn whispered, feeling tears rise in her eyes. "This is good, very good."

❧

The Fontanna homestead was vacated a week later, with everyone returning home to family and friends. Telegrams went out alerting surrounding communities of the new service to be provided to anyone in need. The news made headlines in notable newspapers and magazines.

Preparations had been set for the dance. Mandy, the one surviving servant at the Appleburg estate, helped prepare refreshments. She would stay on indefinitely, preparing food for the patients entering the hospital for care.

Hay bales had been laid out. They used the rough-hewn tables from the first barn dance. Beth Jameston and others set out a delicious array of dishes. Fried chicken, cream gravy, fried cabbage, and summer squash loaded down one table. Another held pork sausage, spare ribs, backbone pie, baked ham, and turnip salad. Desserts included baked custard, chocolate macaroons, mincemeat pie, peanut butter rolls, and sorghum taffy.

A huge pot of sassafras tea was constantly replenished so everyone would have access to the spring tonic. Coffee was also supplied by James. No liquor remained on the premises— Martha had dumped it all out in a nearby ravine.

When all the preparations were complete and the women were taking a few moments to rest, Martha walked to the middle of the barn's hard dirt floor.

"I'd like all the women and young girls to accompany me, please. I've got a little surprise."

A host of baffled comments ran through the crowd. Katelyn smiled as she gripped Carrie's hand and trailed the group. Only their mother stayed behind.

They entered the Victorian mansion with its glossy furnishings and rich decor. Martha led them up the sweeping staircase and on to her bedroom. Katelyn had never been inside a home such as this and believed none of the others had either. What a hospital it would be! While Victorian architecture didn't fit in with the western landscape, a hospital needed to stand out. And this one did just that.

Her eyes were drawn to Martha's canopied bed draped in blue chiffon. There rested some of the most beautiful gowns Katelyn had ever seen. A hush settled on the room as the other women studied the fine garments.

Allowing her eyes to scan the dresses, Katelyn viewed terry velvet gowns decorated with satin ribbons in a variety of colors. Several taffeta carriage dresses rested side by side. Katelyn loved the high necklines and full skirts ornamented with deep flounces, the bottoms trimmed with silk tassels. The shoulders of several were slashed and laced with tasseled silk cord.

Martha broke the silence. "I want each of you to pick out a dress and wear it for the evening."

The women and young girls looked at Martha, then at each other, astonishment showing on their faces.

"Go ahead," Martha coaxed. "And I have rouge and jewels we can use, too. We'll help each other with the latest hairstyles." She giggled. "I know just about all of them," she added without pretension.

At this, the ladies clutched some of the dresses, holding them up to themselves and each other, trying to decide what looked best. Laughter filled the air.

Katelyn drew it all in. It had been so long since joy

abounded in Cimarron. Little Carrie trotted over to her, holding a dress that was at least three times too large for the little girl. Katelyn laughed.

Martha approached. "You can wear that," she said to Carrie. "Let's slip it on over your head. And there are some pumps in the chest."

Martha glanced at Katelyn. "Let her play dress up," she encouraged. "It really is quite fun."

Nodding, Katelyn patted the girl on the head and sent her on her way. "This is really wonderful, Martha," she offered, "to be doing all this."

"It does something for me, Katelyn," Martha confided, "to give instead of receive. Remember what you told me about a week ago? About doing the opposite of what you feel if it's a bad feeling?"

Smiling, Katelyn asked, "Is that what this is all about?"

"Partly," Martha admitted. "But I have discovered that I get a strange feeling, a wonderful feeling, when I give to those in need. I've never quite felt this before, and I love it. Really, I do!"

Stepping toward Martha, Katelyn wrapped her new friend in a tender hug. Martha whispered in Katelyn's ear. "I have something special for you, Katelyn."

She led Katelyn to the armoire and tugged open the door. The garment she withdrew caused a lump to form in Katelyn's throat. Katelyn reached up and touched her neck, as though she could massage the knot away.

"I want you to have this," Martha stated.

"I–I can't."

"Yes, you can," Martha argued. "You saved my life, Katelyn, and the lives of many others. Besides," she continued, "I think it was meant for you all along." She hesitated. "I bought it prematurely; I realize that now. I thought James would surely propose and we'd have a huge wedding with lots of family and friends."

She cleared her throat, dabbed at a tear forming on her

lower lash. "You see, Katelyn, I wasn't even in love with James, nor he with me. I knew that, but I didn't care. Now," she said with a voice full of regret, "I can't believe I actually thought like that. I took so much for granted, even the people around me. Though I knew I was using them to my own benefit, I didn't care."

"You care now, Martha, and that's what counts."

"Yes, I care now. And you know what?"

"What?"

"I am happier now, even though I own so much less. And it's because I've got Jesus in my life and the love of so many people around me. That's where true happiness begins."

Smiling, Katelyn agreed, "Yes, Martha, that's where it begins."

"Go ahead," Martha gestured toward the dress she held. "It's yours."

Slowly, Katelyn retrieved the garment from Martha's arms. Tears fell in steady streams down her cheeks. She ran her free hand over the white satin. Embroidered white satin flounces interchanged with pleated chiffon flounces. A bandeau of white silk lilac and orange blossoms hosted a veil of tulle illusion. Short white kid gloves completed the ensemble. An image of white roses, white lilies, lilac, and orange blossoms formed in Katelyn's mind as the perfect bouquet for her wedding ceremony.

She focused on Martha again, who wore one of the largest smiles Katelyn had ever seen on her face. "I–I don't know what to say."

"Don't say anything," said Martha. "Just accept the gift, from my heart to yours." A woman called her name.

"Better get started," Martha said. "The men of Cimarron are in for quite a treat. Don't you think?"

"Oh yes," Katelyn answered. *And James is in for a treat when he sees this gown on me for the first time,* she thought. Never in her lifetime had she expected something like this. Poverty had plagued her and her family all their lives.

Suddenly she owned the most beautiful gown she'd ever seen.

But Katelyn didn't change into a gown as the others had. She remained in her blue paisley dress and followed the others back to the party.

❧

A hush rose inside the barn. All music ceased as the Cimarron women, one by one, strolled onto the dance floor. When the last one entered, applause and shouts of approval rent the air. The music began again.

James made his way to Katelyn and sat on a bale of hay next to her. "This is very different from the last barn dance," he observed.

Katelyn smiled at him, eyes gleaming. "I wasn't able to attend," she responded. "So, I have nothing to compare it to."

"Trust me, there's no comparison." James threw his glance around the room, watching the dancers. "I left the last dance early because I grew worried about my father. He was sick. Others never showed because they already had the smallpox, though we didn't know it at the time."

"Guess I'm glad that I wasn't here."

Touching her hand with his strong fingers, James gazed on her again. "It's fitting that we should end on this note, since we began on it."

"I agree." Katelyn threw James a lopsided grin.

Her mother approached them, carrying two tumblers in her hands. "Here," she instructed. "Sassafras tea. Drink up."

Both Katelyn and James laughed.

"I'm a bit tired of sassafras, Mama," said Katelyn.

"Me, too," James added, smiling and sipping the brew obediently.

Her mother's next words caught Katelyn off guard. "Daughter, they want you to sing for them."

"Who?"

"Everybody."

"But. . .I. . ."

James gave her a little shove. "Yes, you can," he told her. "You have a beautiful voice, Katelyn. They don't call you 'The Song of the Cimarron' for nothing."

"I'm honored."

"So," he coaxed, "you'd better live up to your new title."

Katelyn managed a nervous smile.

"Come on," her mother urged, gripping Katelyn by the hand and tugging her to her feet. The crowd applauded.

Approaching the raised platform, Katelyn stepped up. The fiddler provided her with a stool. Then he began to play "Little Brown Jug," to which the banjo player and the old-timer on the harmonica joined in. Another played the juice harp. Dancers swarmed the floor to perform waltzes and square dances.

Katelyn hummed at first, attempting to loosen the muscles constricting her throat. Then she mouthed the words, softly at first. Soon, though, her voice rang through the air with a birdlike quality.

James watched on, so proud of the woman who had agreed to be his life partner and so thankful that God had allowed it to be so. Then he stood.

She had just completed a verse when Katelyn saw James approach. When he waved his hand in the air, the muscles in Katelyn's throat tightened. *What are you doing?*

Turning to face the audience, James raised his voice. "I'd like everybody's attention," he said. He looked directly at Katelyn. "Katy, come here."

For a moment, Katelyn didn't move. She felt frozen in place. Only her eyes shifted as they viewed the participants in the barn dance watching her.

Laughing, James approached and gripped her gently by the upper right arm. "A little shy?" He chuckled when Katelyn still didn't budge. "Come on," he coaxed. "It's okay. It'll be over in a minute."

"What?" Katelyn whispered. "What will be over?"

"You'll see. Now come on to this bale of hay."

Allowing herself to be led by the arm, Katelyn felt her cheeks grow hot. Did he want her to stand on a bale and sing? Certainly not!

"James? What's going on?" she asked as he lifted her to where her feet rested on the square bundle. When he climbed on with her, she felt her heart race.

Then he spoke loudly. "Thank you for your attention," James began. "I want to say, first, that we, Katelyn and I, are grateful for all the help the people of Cimarron provided. We couldn't have survived without each other," he added. "It was by the efforts of all that Cimarron will continue to prosper, continue to be a town, a community."

A murmur of agreement mixed with James's words.

"I think it's brought us all closer together!" Beth Jameston shouted.

Several "amens" showed that others agreed.

"Anyhow," James continued, "we made it by the grace of God. Yes, we lost loved ones and dear friends, but we still have each other. And we have a future! All of us!"

The room buzzed as people hugged one another, feeling the charge of the moment. James turned to look down at Katelyn, smiled, then drew his attention back on his task.

Confusion caused Katelyn's forehead to wrinkle. Couldn't all of this have been said without them standing on a block of hay? She started to step down, but James caught her by the skirt of her dress.

"Not yet," he told her. "I have one more announcement to make!" he shouted, gaining the attention of the onlookers once again.

Katelyn drew in a deep breath. *Announcement?* She was beginning to understand.

James wrapped an arm around Katelyn's shoulders and hugged her to him. "Katelyn and I extend a special invitation to all of you in attendance here to our. . .wedding!"

An explosion of shouts and laughter roared through the room like a sudden storm. James laughed hard and jumped down. He lifted Katelyn off and swung her around in his arms. The musicians struck up a lively tune. People approached and gathered around, congratulating the couple with pats on the back and encouraging words.

A warm smile stretched across Katelyn's lips. "I love you, James," she whispered, her eyes sparkling.

"I love you, too, Katy girl. I love you, too."

They danced the night away.

A Letter To Our Readers

Dear Reader:

In order that we might better contribute to your reading enjoyment, we would appreciate your taking a few minutes to respond to the following questions. When completed, please return to the following:

Rebecca Germany, Managing Editor
Heartsong Presents
PO Box 719
Uhrichsville, Ohio 44683

1. Did you enjoy reading *Song of the Cimarron?*
   ❏ Very much. I would like to see more books
      by this author!
   ❏ Moderately
      I would have enjoyed it more if _____

   _____

2. Are you a member of **Heartsong Presents**? ❏Yes ❏No
   If no, where did you purchase this book?_____

   _____

3. What influenced your decision to purchase this
   book? (Check those that apply.)

   ❏ Cover   ❏ Back cover copy

   ❏ Title   ❏ Friends

   ❏ Publicity   ❏ Other_____

4. How would you rate, on a scale from 1 (poor) to 5
   (superior), the cover design?_____

5. On a scale from 1 (poor) to 10 (superior), please rate the following elements.

    ___Heroine   ___Plot

    ___Hero   ___Inspirational theme

    ___Setting   ___Secondary characters

6. What settings would you like to see covered in **Heartsong Presents** books?_____

_____

_____

7. What are some inspirational themes you would like to see treated in future books?_____

_____

_____

8. Would you be interested in reading other **Heartsong Presents** titles? ❑ Yes   ❑ No

9. Please check your age range:
    ❑ Under 18   ❑ 18-24   ❑ 25-34
    ❑ 35-45   ❑ 46-55   ❑ Over 55

10. How many hours per week do you read? _____

Name _____

Occupation_____

Address _____

City_____ State_____Zip _____

Most holidays last only a short while,

but the romance of Christmas lingers on. It is the season for mistletoe and crackling fires, for stolen kisses and ecstatic reunions, for blushing glances and the heart-pounding magic of love. Recapture the wonder of Christmas in these two brand new four-in-one novella collections.

Remember Christmases long gone past in *A Nostalgic Noel*—featuring *Kay Cornelius, Rebecca Germany, Darlene Mindrup,* and *Colleen L. Reece.*

Celebrate today with *Season of Love*—featuring *Yvonne Lehman, Lorree Lough, Tracie Peterson,* and *Debra White Smith.*

Both: Trade Paperback, 352 Pages

·····Heart♥ng·····

HEARTSONG PRESENTS TITLES AVAILABLE NOW:

(If ordering from this page, please remember to include it with the order form.)

········· Presents ·········

Great Inspirational Romance at a Great Price!

Heartsong Presents books are inspirational romances in contemporary and historical settings, designed to give you an enjoyable, spirit-lifting reading experience. You can choose wonderfully written titles from some of today's best authors like Peggy Darty, Sally Laity, Tracie Peterson, Colleen L. Reece, Lauraine Snelling, and many others.

When ordering quantities less than twelve, above titles are $2.95 each.
Not all titles may be available at time of order.

SEND TO: Heartsong Presents Reader's Service
P.O. Box 719, Uhrichsville, Ohio 44683

Please send me the items checked above. I am enclosing $_____.
(please add $1.00 to cover postage per order. OH add 6.25% tax. NJ add 6%). Send check or money order, no cash or C.O.D.s, please.
To place a credit card order, call 1-800-847-8270.

NAME _____

ADDRESS _____

CITY/STATE_____ ZIP _____

HPS 12-98

Hearts♥ng Presents
Love Stories Are Rated G!

That's for godly, gratifying, and of course, great! If you love a thrilling love story, but don't appreciate the sordidness of some popular paperback romances, **Heartsong Presents** is for you. In fact, **Heartsong Presents** is the *only inspirational romance book club*, the only one featuring love stories where Christian faith is the primary ingredient in a marriage relationship.

Sign up today to receive your first set of four, never before published Christian romances. Send no money now; you will receive a bill with the first shipment. You may cancel at any time without obligation, and if you aren't completely satisfied with any selection, you may return the books for an immediate refund!

Imagine. . .four new romances every four weeks—two historical, two contemporary—with men and women like you who long to meet the one God has chosen as the love of their lives. . .all for the low price of $9.97 postpaid.

To join, simply complete the coupon below and mail to the address provided. **Heartsong Presents** romances are rated G for another reason: They'll arrive *Godspeed!*
